War

Other Books in the Issues on Trial Series:

War

Sylvia Engdahl, Book Editor

GREENHAVEN PRESS
A part of Gale, Cengage Learning

GALE
CENGAGE Learning™

Detroit • New York • San Francisco • New Haven, Conn • Waterville, Maine • London

GALE
CENGAGE Learning·

Christine Nasso, *Publisher*
Elizabeth Des Chenes, *Managing Editor*

© 2010 Greenhaven Press, a part of Gale, Cengage Learning

For more information, contact:
Greenhaven Press
27500 Drake Rd.
Farmington Hills, MI 48331-3535
Or you can visit our Internet site at gale.cengage.com.

For product information and technology assistance, contact us at

Gale Customer Support, 1-800-877-4253
For permission to use material from this text or product, submit all requests online at www.cengage.com/permissions

Further permissions questions can be emailed to permissionrequest@cengage.com

Articles in Greenhaven Press anthologies are often edited for length to meet page requirements. In addition, original titles of these works are changed to clearly present the main thesis and to explicitly indicate the author's opinion. Every effort is made to ensure that Greenhaven Press accurately reflects the original intent of the authors. Every effort has been made to trace the owners of copyrighted material.

Cover Image William James Warren/Science Faction/CORBIS.

LIBRARY OF CONGRESS CATALOGING-IN-PUBLICATION DATA

War / Sylvia Engdahl, book editor.
  p. cm. -- (Issues on trial)
  Includes bibliographical references and index.
  ISBN 978-0-7377-4949-6 (hardcover)
  1. War--Moral and ethical aspects--Case studies--Juvenile literature. I. Engdahl, Sylvia.
  U22.W275 2010
  343.73'01541--dc22
                                                                    2010007872

Printed in the United States of America
1 2 3 4 5 6 7 14 13 12 11 10

Contents

A law professor argues that evidence shows that, contrary to the belief of critics, Japanese Americans who were relocated were not treated shamefully, that at the time it occurred there was espionage known to authorities with access to classified information, and that there was no way the innocent could be distinguished from those who posed a threat.

Chapter 2: Refusing a Stay of Execution to Cold War Spies

A recent article about the Rosenberg case explains what led up to the trial, the public reaction to it, and how historians view it today.

Chapter 3: Affirming That Conscientious Objectors Must Oppose All War

Chapter 4: Trying Foreign Terrorists by Military Commission

A law professor who formerly worked for the government points out that Congress, in passing legislation
overriding the Court's decision in *Hamdan v. Rumsfeld*,
has restored the president's power to manage the war on
terror and has made clear that the courts must stay out of
it.

Foreword

The U.S. courts have long served as a battleground for the most highly charged and contentious issues of the time. Divisive matters are often brought into the legal system by activists who feel strongly for their cause and demand an official resolution. Indeed, subjects that give rise to intense emotions or involve closely held religious or moral beliefs lay at the heart of the most polemical court rulings in history. One such case was *Brown v. Board of Education* (1954), which ended racial segregation in schools. Prior to *Brown*, the courts had held that blacks could be forced to use separate facilities as long as these facilities were equal to that of whites.

For years many groups had opposed segregation based on religious, moral, and legal grounds. Educators produced heartfelt testimony that segregated schooling greatly disadvantaged black children. They noted that in comparison to whites, blacks received a substandard education in deplorable conditions. Religious leaders such as Martin Luther King Jr. preached that the harsh treatment of blacks was immoral and unjust. Many involved in civil rights law, such as Thurgood Marshall, called for equal protection of all people under the law, as their study of the Constitution had indicated that segregation was illegal and un-American. Whatever their motivation for ending the practice, and despite the threats they received from segregationists, these ardent activists remained unwavering in their cause.

Those fighting against the integration of schools were mainly white southerners who did not believe that whites and blacks should intermingle. Blacks were subordinate to whites, they maintained, and society had to resist any attempt to break down strict color lines. Some white southerners charged that segregated schooling was *not* hindering blacks' education. For example, Virginia attorney general J. Lindsay Almond asserted, "With the help and the sympathy and the love and respect of the white people of the South, the colored man has risen under that educational process to a place of eminence and respect throughout the nation. It has served him well." So when the Supreme Court ruled against the segregationists in *Brown*, the South responded with vociferous cries of protest. Even government leaders criticized the decision. The governor of Arkansas, Orval Faubus, stated that he would not "be a party to any attempt to force acceptance of change to which the people are so overwhelmingly opposed." Indeed, resistance to integration was so great that when black students arrived at the formerly all-white Central High School in Arkansas, federal troops had to be dispatched to quell a threatening mob of protesters.

Nevertheless, the *Brown* decision was enforced and the South integrated its schools. In this instance, the Court, while not settling the issue to everyone's satisfaction, functioned as an instrument of progress by forcing a major social change. Historian David Halberstam observes that the *Brown* ruling "deprived segregationist practices of their moral legitimacy. . . . It was therefore perhaps the single most important moment of the decade, the moment that separated the old order from the new and helped create the tumultuous era just arriving." Considered one of the most important victories for civil rights, *Brown* paved the way for challenges to racial segregation in many areas, including on public buses and in restaurants.

In examining *Brown*, it becomes apparent that the courts play an influential role—and face an arduous challenge—in shaping the debate over emotionally charged social issues. Judges must balance competing interests, keeping in mind the high stakes and intense emotions on both sides. As exemplified by *Brown*, judicial decisions often upset the status quo and initiate significant changes in society. Greenhaven Press's Issues on Trial series captures the controversy surrounding influential court rulings and explores the social ramifications of such decisions from varying perspectives. Each anthology highlights one social issue—such as the death penalty, students' rights, or wartime civil liberties. Each volume then focuses on key historical and contemporary court cases that helped mold the issue as we know it today. The books include a compendium of primary sources—court rulings, dissents, and immediate reactions to the rulings—as well as secondary sources from experts in the field, people involved in the cases, legal analysts, and other commentators opining on the implications and legacy of the chosen cases. An annotated table of contents, an in-depth introduction, and prefaces that overview each case all provide context as readers delve into the topic at hand. To help students fully probe the subject, each volume contains book and periodical bibliographies, a comprehensive index, and a list of organizations to contact. With these features, the Issues on Trial series offers a well-rounded perspective on the courts' role in framing society's thorniest, most impassioned debates.

Introduction

One of the most difficult issues any free society has to face is the balancing of liberty and safety. In principle, a free society is one in which the right to individual freedom is established by law—in the United States, by the U.S. Constitution and its amendments. But there are occasions when to allow total freedom would endanger the public at large. Most obviously, this is true in the case of violent crime, which everyone agrees must be banned. Far more troubling questions of balance arise during wartime.

In his book *War and Liberty: An American Dilemma*, Geoffrey R. Stone writes, "War poses threats that do not exist in peacetime, and there is every reason to think hard about whether we can afford to preserve our liberties in time of war. But we must also be wary of the perils of war fever. Wartime emotions run high." It is often difficult to draw the line between decisions based on a realistic assessment of danger and those based on unwarranted fears.

Many people believe that to limit individual liberty in the name of national security is self-defeating if the goal is to defend freedom. They cite Benjamin Franklin's well-known statement "Those who would give up essential Liberty, to purchase a little temporary Safety, deserve neither Liberty nor Safety"— often misquoting it to the extent of leaving out the qualifier "temporary." But few of these people believe that it would be better for all freedom to be destroyed by defeat in a war against a totalitarian power than to accept restrictions truly necessary to prevent such a defeat. The controversies arise through disagreement about the degree of necessity and the extent of the specific threat involved.

Another often-quoted saying is "The Constitution is not a suicide pact." Although sometimes attributed to Abraham Lincoln, this is actually derived from Supreme Court justice Robert H. Jackson's dissenting opinion in *Terminiello v. Chicago* (1949), a free-speech case in which he wrote: "There is danger that, if the Court does not temper its doctrinaire logic with a little practical wisdom, it will convert the constitutional Bill of Rights into a suicide pact." He feared that to allow radical Fascists and Communists to incite demonstrations by inflammatory speech would reduce the power of local governments to prevent widespread violence. The phrase is most often used, however, in the context of preventing serious danger to the nation.

The first time the U.S. government limited liberty for the sake of security was with the Sedition Act of 1798, which forbade conspiracy "with intent to oppose any measure or measures of the government of the United States" and publication of "any false, scandalous and malicious writing" against the government. The nation was then embroiled in an undeclared war with France and feared invasion; also, the political party in power felt that the more liberal ideas of the opposition party might lead to the kind of violence that the French Revolution had produced in that country. A number of newspaper editors were convicted of sedition, and their papers were shut down. Once the conflict with France cooled, however, public objection to the law brought about the victory of the opposition party and the election of Thomas Jefferson to the presidency.

One of the most famous denials of constitutional rights in American history occurred during the Civil War, when president Abraham Lincoln suspended the writ of habeas corpus, the principle of law that prevents a prisoner from being held indefinitely without being charged with a crime. The Constitution guarantees this right, but also allows exceptions; it states: "The privilege of the writ of habeas corpus shall not be suspended, unless when in cases of rebellion or invasion the public safety may require it." On several occasions Lincoln believed that public safety did require the arrest of people who were merely potential threats, but this was widely questioned even at the time, and his action has generally been viewed as an unfortunate mistake.

A second Sedition Act was passed in 1918, during World War I. It prohibited the use in wartime of "disloyal, profane, scurrilous, or abusive language" about the U.S. form of government, the Constitution, the flag, or the armed forces, and was upheld along with the Espionage Act by the Supreme Court in *Debs v. United States* (1919). Earlier that year justice Oliver Wendell Holmes had written in *Schenck v. United States* (1919)—a case in which the Court affirmed the conviction of radicals who had published an antidraft pamphlet—that "when a nation is at war, many things that might be said in time of peace are such a hindrance to its effort . . . that no Court could regard them as protected by any constitutional right." Because of these decisions, many U.S. citizens were imprisoned for antiwar protests under the law, which was repealed in 1920 following its abuse by government officials.

Since then, the banning of free speech—except to prevent the disclosure of classified (secret) information or the incitement of violence against the government—has not been viewed as justified even in wartime; widespread dissent during the Vietnam War was tolerated. But there have been other abridgments of individual rights. In every case, some people believed that the government's action was necessary to counter a real threat, while others felt that there was no actual danger and that the action arose from prejudice or was taken solely for political reasons. The situation was complicated by the fact that government officials with high security clearances possessed information not known to the public, a factor that is often overlooked. Today, there is still disagreement about these incidents. It appears likely that the dangers were not as great as they seemed at the time, but the people who acted from fear did not have the benefit of hindsight.

Most deprivations of personal liberty have gained little support from Americans except at the height of emotion over an immediate threat. The military draft is an example of one that has been more consistently accepted. It has sometimes been argued that the draft is a violation of the Thirteenth Amendment's prohibition of "involuntary servitude." The wording of the amendment would certainly imply that it is; however, while in general there is disagreement among jurists as to how strictly the words of the Constitution should be interpreted, on some issues a literal interpretation is ruled out by what many view as common sense. As Justice Holmes famously stated in *Schenck*, "The most stringent protection of free speech would not protect a man in falsely shouting fire in a theatre and causing a panic."

Moreover, a provision's original intent is always considered. The courts have viewed the draft as permissible under the government's constitutionally authorized power to raise armies, as well as sanctioned by the fact that the Thirteenth Amendment's authors clearly did not mean it to be prohibited. In *Butler v. Perry* (1916) the Supreme Court stated that "the term 'involuntary servitude' was intended to cover those forms of compulsory labor akin to African slavery which, in practical operation, would tend to produce like undesirable results. It introduced no novel doctrine ... and certainly was not intended to interdict enforcement of those duties which individuals owe to the state, such as services in the army, militia, on the jury, etc."

A little later, the Court unanimously ruled on the draft in *Arver v. United States* (1918); its opinion declared, "As we are unable to conceive upon what theory the exaction by government from the citizen of the performance of his supreme and noble duty of contributing to the defense of the rights and honor of the nation, as the result of a war declared by the great representative body of the people, can be said to be the imposition of involuntary servitude in violation of the prohibitions of the Thirteenth Amendment, we are constrained to the conclusion that the contention to that effect is refuted by its mere statement."

Some people disagree with this ruling, and occasionally it has been pointed out that since not all military action is "the result of a war declared by the great representative body of the people" (i.e., by Congress), it should not be considered applicable in every case. Legally, however, it is binding. For Congress to pass draft laws is thus not unconstitutional. The main controversies regarding them have concerned who shall be exempted from the draft or allowed to perform alternate service as a conscientious objector. For conscientious objectors, the problem of principle versus public safety is especially acute because it is a decision each must make personally.

Few people would fight voluntarily if they did not believe they were defending their country or helping to eliminate a long-term threat to world peace. Pacifists hold that it is wrong to fight even for these reasons, and the law exempts them from combat. There are also people who would fight if the nation were attacked, but not in a situation where they do not agree that a threat to it is involved. Should they too be exempt? The Supreme Court has ruled that under current law, they are not; that is one of the cases included in this book.

The underlying issue in such cases is not just a matter of conscientious objection to war. It is the more fundamental problem of balance between individual freedom and the responsibility of a democratic government to protect its people against current or future violence. There is no simple way to determine this balance, and because people's perceptions of threats differ, there can never be full agreement in any particular situation. It can only be recognized that in wartime, as at other times, both liberty and safety are important, and neither should be allowed to preclude consideration of the other.

CHAPTER 1

Relocating Japanese Americans During World War II

Case Overview

Korematsu v. United States (1944)

In 1941 the American naval base at Pearl Harbor, Hawaii, was attacked by Japan, marking the entry of the United States into World War II. It was a surprise attack that profoundly shocked America. Those who lived on the West Coast were particularly frightened, for only the Pacific Ocean lay between them and Japan, which had attacked Hawaii from aircraft carriers and submarines. It was not the same as in later years, when the advent of missiles made every part of the United States as vulnerable to enemy attack as any other. Furthermore, many people of Japanese ancestry lived on the West Coast, which was not only the closest area to Japan, but the location of important aircraft factories, shipyards, and other defense facilities. There were air-raid drills, and people were asked to put blackout curtains on their windows. It was a nervous time for everyone.

The Japanese Americans in the region had kept many elements of their own culture rather than allowing themselves to be completely assimilated into American culture, even though the younger ones, having been born in the United States, were American citizens. Some children had been sent to Japan for education and others to Japanese-language schools in addition to public school, where they were taught to respect the traditions of Japan. For this reason, American military authorities considered them suspect, although the vast majority were loyal to the United States and were appalled by the Japanese attack. It was felt that a few might be involved in spying for Japan or even in sabotage, and there was no way to distinguish those few from all the others. Therefore, the government issued an order requiring everyone of Japanese ancestry to leave the West Coast states and move somewhere else.

Today, this is almost universally regarded as a shameful episode in American history, and in fact in 1988 the U.S. government issued the first of several formal apologies to Japanese Americans for it, along with the payment of financial reparations to survivors. Ordering American citizens not personally suspected of any wrongdoing to leave their homes, and arresting them if they refused, would be unthinkable now. It is commonly said that they were imprisoned in internment camps, but this is not entirely true; they were free to leave the area on their own, although those who did not do so immediately were sent to temporary camps and, eventually, since they had nowhere else to go, to relocation centers set up by the government. They could leave those centers on condition that they not return to the West Coast, but—since they had been forced to abandon their property—most had no money to settle elsewhere and were detained in the relocation centers until near the end of the war.

Not surprisingly, even at the time there were some people who believed that forcibly excluding American citizens from their home states was unconstitutional. And there were some Japanese Americans who refused to comply. A young man named Fred Korematsu was one of these; when he was found still in California, he was arrested for disobeying the order and sent to jail. With the help of lawyers who believed his rights had been violated he took his case to court, and eventually it reached the Supreme Court. The Court's landmark decision is now widely considered to be one of the worst it has ever made.

By a 6 to 3 majority the Court ruled against Korematsu, maintaining that the exclusion of Japanese Americans from the West Coast was a matter of military necessity. Although it made plain that the order had been issued because of their connection to Japan and not merely their race, one of the dissenters and many critics nevertheless called it racist. Critics also pointed out that there had been no cases of espionage or sabotage involving Japanese Americans. In any event, the Court refused to uphold the constitutional rights to which innocent American citizens are normally entitled.

Many years later it was discovered that government officials had been dishonest in the evidence they gave the Supreme Court about the threat of espionage (although some scholars point out that there was indeed evidence known at the time only to the President and others with the highest security clearance). Fred Korematsu's case was reopened in a U.S. district court, and his conviction was overturned. He became an activist for the rights of Japanese Americans and others, and in 1998 he was awarded the Medal of Freedom, the nation's highest civilian honor. When he died in 2005 at the age of eighty-six, he was widely eulogized as a hero.

"All legal restrictions which curtail the civil rights of a single racial group are immediately suspect. That is not to say that all such restrictions are unconstitutional."

Majority Opinion: Military Authority to Relocate Innocent Citizens During Wartime Is Constitutional

Hugo Black

Hugo Black was a justice of the Supreme Court from 1937 to 1971, the fourth-longest-serving member in its history. He was noted for a strict interpretation of the Constitution's text. In the following majority opinion he wrote for the Court in Korematsu v. United States, *he argues that legal restrictions on the rights of a single racial group must be subjected to rigid scrutiny but that public necessity may sometimes justify them. In a previous case the Court upheld a curfew imposed on Japanese Americans as a necessary step to prevent espionage and sabotage, and the exclusion order, too, is a military imperative, he contends. He points out, however, that the Japanese Americans were excluded not because of racial prejudice but because the nation was at war with Japan and there was evidence of disloyalty on the part of some citizens of Japanese ancestry. Nor was the Court passing judgment on the issue of relocation centers, since some sent to relocation centers were released on condition that they remain outside the exclusion area and Fred Korematsu's only offense was his refusal to leave that area.*

Hugo Black, majority opinion, *Korematsu v. United States*, United States Supreme Court, December 18, 1944. Reproduced by permission.

The petitioner [Fred Korematsu], an American citizen of Japanese descent, was convicted in a federal district court for remaining in San Leandro, California, a "Military Area," contrary to Civilian Exclusion Order No. 34 of the Commanding General of the Western Command, U.S. Army, which directed that, after May 9, 1942, all persons of Japanese ancestry should be excluded from that area. No question was raised as to petitioner's loyalty to the United States. The Circuit Court of Appeals affirmed, and the importance of the constitutional question involved caused us to grant certiorari [review].

It should be noted, to begin with, that all legal restrictions which curtail the civil rights of a single racial group are immediately suspect. That is not to say that all such restrictions are unconstitutional. It is to say that courts must subject them to the most rigid scrutiny. Pressing public necessity may sometimes justify the existence of such restrictions; racial antagonism never can.

In the instant [present] case, prosecution of the petitioner was begun by information charging violation of an Act of Congress, of March 21, 1942, which provides that

> ... whoever shall enter, remain in, leave, or commit any act in any military area or military zone prescribed, under the authority of an Executive order of the President, by the Secretary of War, or by any military commander designated by the Secretary of War, contrary to the restrictions applicable to any such area or zone or contrary to the order of the Secretary of War or any such military commander, shall, if it appears that he knew or should have known of the existence and extent of the restrictions or order and that his act was in violation thereof, be guilty of a misdemeanor and upon conviction shall be liable to a fine of not to exceed $5,000 or to imprisonment for not more than one year, or both, for each offense.

Exclusion Order No. 34, which the petitioner knowingly and admittedly violated, was one of a number of military orders and proclamations, all of which were substantially based upon Executive Order No. 9066. That order, issued after we were at war with Japan, declared that "the successful prosecution of the war requires every possible protection against espionage and against sabotage to national defense material, national defense premises, and national defense utilities. . . ."

Hirabayashi v. United States

One of the series of orders and proclamations, a curfew order, which, like the exclusion order here, was promulgated pursuant to Executive Order 9066, subjected all persons of Japanese ancestry in prescribed West Coast military areas to remain in their residences from 8 p.m. to 6 a.m. As is the case with the exclusion order here, that prior curfew order was designed as a "protection against espionage and against sabotage." In *Hirabayashi v. United States*, we sustained a conviction obtained for violation of the curfew order. The Hirabayashi conviction and this one thus rest on the same 1942 Congressional Act and the same basic executive and military orders, all of which orders were aimed at the twin dangers of espionage and sabotage.

The 1942 Act was attacked in the *Hirabayashi* case as an unconstitutional delegation of power; it was contended that the curfew order and other orders on which it rested were beyond the war powers of the Congress, the military authorities, and of the President, as Commander in Chief of the Army, and, finally, that to apply the curfew order against none but citizens of Japanese ancestry amounted to a constitutionally prohibited discrimination solely on account of race. To these questions, we gave the serious consideration which their importance justified. We upheld the curfew order as an exercise of the power of the government to take steps necessary to prevent espionage and sabotage in an area threatened by Japanese attack.

In the light of the principles we announced in the *Hiraba-yashi* case, we are unable to conclude that it was beyond the war power of Congress and the Executive to exclude those of Japanese ancestry from the West Coast war area at the time they did. True, exclusion from the area in which one's home is located is a far greater deprivation than constant confinement to the home from 8 p.m. to 6 a.m. Nothing short of apprehension by the proper military authorities of the gravest imminent danger to the public safety can constitutionally justify either. But exclusion from a threatened area, no less than curfew, has a definite and close relationship to the prevention of espionage and sabotage. The military authorities, charged with the primary responsibility of defending our shores, concluded that curfew provided inadequate protection and ordered exclusion. They did so, as pointed out in our *Hirabayashi* opinion, in accordance with Congressional authority to the military to say who should, and who should not, remain in the threatened areas.

In this case, the petitioner challenges the assumptions upon which we rested our conclusions in the *Hirabayashi* case. He also urges that, by May, 1942, when Order No. 34 was promulgated, all danger of Japanese invasion of the West Coast had disappeared. After careful consideration of these contentions, we are compelled to reject them.

Here, as in the *Hirabayashi* case,

. . . we cannot reject as unfounded the judgment of the military authorities and of Congress that there were disloyal members of that population, whose number and strength could not be precisely and quickly ascertained. We cannot say that the war-making branches of the Government did not have ground for believing that, in a critical hour, such persons could not readily be isolated and separately dealt with, and constituted a menace to the national defense and safety which demanded that prompt and adequate measures be taken to guard against it.

A Military Imperative

Like curfew, exclusion of those of Japanese origin was deemed necessary because of the presence of an unascertained number of disloyal members of the group, most of whom we have no doubt were loyal to this country. It was because we could not reject the finding of the military authorities that it was impossible to bring about an immediate segregation of the disloyal from the loyal that we sustained the validity of the curfew order as applying to the whole group. In the instant case, temporary exclusion of the entire group was rested by the military on the same ground. The judgment that exclusion of the whole group was, for the same reason, a military imperative answers the contention that the exclusion was in the nature of group punishment based on antagonism to those of Japanese origin. That there were members of the group who retained loyalties to Japan has been confirmed by investigations made subsequent to the exclusion. Approximately five thousand American citizens of Japanese ancestry refused to swear unqualified allegiance to the United States and to renounce allegiance to the Japanese Emperor, and several thousand evacuees requested repatriation to Japan.

We uphold the exclusion order as of the time it was made and when the petitioner violated it. In doing so, we are not unmindful of the hardships imposed by it upon a large group of American citizens. But hardships are part of war, and war is an aggregation of hardships. All citizens alike, both in and out of uniform, feel the impact of war in greater or lesser measure. Citizenship has its responsibilities, as well as its privileges, and, in time of war, the burden is always heavier. Compulsory exclusion of large groups of citizens from their homes, except under circumstances of direst emergency and peril, is inconsistent with our basic governmental institutions. But when, under conditions of modern warfare, our shores are threatened by hostile forces, the power to protect must be commensurate with the threatened danger.

It is argued that, on May 30, 1942, the date the petitioner was charged with remaining in the prohibited area, there were conflicting orders outstanding, forbidding him both to leave the area and to remain there. Of course, a person cannot be convicted for doing the very thing which it is a crime to fail to do. But the outstanding orders here contained no such contradictory commands.

There was an order issued March 27, 1942, which prohibited petitioner and others of Japanese ancestry from leaving the area, but its effect was specifically limited in time "until and to the extent that a future proclamation or order should so permit or direct." That "future order," the one for violation of which petitioner was convicted, was issued May 3, 1942, and it did "direct" exclusion from the area of all persons of Japanese ancestry before 12 o'clock noon, May 9; furthermore, it contained a warning that all such persons found in the prohibited area would be liable to punishment under the March 21, 1942, Act of Congress. Consequently, the only order in effect touching the petitioner's being in the area on May 30, 1942, the date specified in the information against him, was the May 3 order which prohibited his remaining there, and it was that same order which he stipulated in his trial that he had violated, knowing of its existence. There is therefore no basis for the argument that, on May 30, 1942, he was subject to punishment, under the March 27 and May 3 orders, whether he remained in or left the area.

Detention Not the Issue Here

It does appear, however, that, on May 9, the effective date of the exclusion order, the military authorities had already determined that the evacuation should be effected by assembling together and placing under guard all those of Japanese ancestry at central points, designated as "assembly centers," in order "to insure the orderly evacuation and resettlement of Japanese voluntarily migrating from Military Area No. 1, to restrict and regulate such migration."

And on May 19, 1942, eleven days before the time petitioner was charged with unlawfully remaining in the area, Civilian Restrictive Order No. 1, provided for detention of those of Japanese ancestry in assembly or relocation centers. It is now argued that the validity of the exclusion order cannot be considered apart from the orders requiring him, after departure from the area, to report and to remain in an assembly or relocation center. The contention is that we must treat these separate orders as one and inseparable; that, for this reason, if detention in the assembly or relocation center would have illegally deprived the petitioner of his Liberty, the exclusion order and his conviction under it cannot stand.

We are thus being asked to pass at this time upon the whole subsequent detention program in both assembly and relocation centers, although the only issues framed at the trial related to petitioner's remaining in the prohibited area in violation of the exclusion order. Had petitioner here left the prohibited area and gone to an assembly center, we cannot say, either as a matter of fact or law, that his presence in that center would have resulted in his detention in a relocation center. Some who did report to the assembly center were not sent to relocation centers, but were released upon condition that they remain outside the prohibited zone until the military orders were modified or lifted. This illustrates that they pose different problems, and may be governed by different principles. The lawfulness of one does not necessarily determine the lawfulness of the others. This is made clear when we analyze the requirements of the separate provisions of the separate orders. These separate requirements were that those of Japanese ancestry (1) depart from the area; (2) report to and temporarily remain in an assembly center; (3) go under military control to a relocation center, there to remain for an indeterminate period until released conditionally or unconditionally by the military authorities. Each of these requirements, it will be noted, imposed distinct duties in connection with the separate steps in a complete evacuation program. Had Congress directly incorporated into one Act the language of these separate orders, and provided sanctions for their violations, disobedience of any one would have constituted a separate offense. There is no reason why violations of these orders, insofar as they were promulgated pursuant to Congressional enactment, should not be treated as separate offenses. . . .

Since the petitioner has not been convicted of failing to report or to remain in an assembly or relocation center, we cannot in this case determine the validity of those separate provisions of the order. It is sufficient here for us to pass upon the order which petitioner violated. To do more would be to go beyond the issues raised, and to decide momentous questions not contained within the framework of the pleadings or the evidence in this case. It will be time enough to decide the serious constitutional issues which petitioner seeks to raise when an assembly or relocation order is applied or is certain to be applied to him, and we have its terms before us.

Some of the members of the Court are of the view that evacuation and detention in an Assembly Center were inseparable. After May 3, 1942, the date of Exclusion Order No. 34, Korematsu was under compulsion to leave the area not as he would choose, but via an Assembly Center. The Assembly Center was conceived as a part of the machinery for group evacuation. The power to exclude includes the power to do it by force if necessary. And any forcible measure must necessarily entail some degree of detention or restraint, whatever method of removal is selected. But whichever view is taken, it results in holding that the order under which petitioner was convicted was valid.

It is said that we are dealing here with the case of imprisonment of a citizen in a concentration camp solely because of his ancestry, without evidence or inquiry concerning his loyalty and good disposition towards the United States. Our task would be simple, our duty clear, were this a case involving the imprisonment of a loyal citizen in a concentration camp because of racial prejudice. Regardless of the true nature of the assembly and relocation centers—and we deem it unjustifiable to call them concentration camps, with all the ugly connotations that term implies—we are dealing specifically with nothing but an exclusion order. To cast this case into outlines of racial prejudice, without reference to the real military dangers which were presented, merely confuses the issue. Korematsu was not excluded from the Military Area because of hostility to him or his race. He was excluded because we are at war with the Japanese Empire, because the properly constituted military authorities feared an invasion of our West Coast and felt constrained to take proper security measures, because they decided that the military urgency of the situation demanded that all citizens of Japanese ancestry be segregated from the West Coast temporarily, and, finally, because Congress, reposing its confidence in this time of war in our military leaders—as inevitably it must—determined that they should have the power to do just this. There was evidence of disloyalty on the part of some, the military authorities considered that the need for action was great, and time was short. We cannot—by availing ourselves of the calm perspective of hindsight—now say that, at that time, these actions were unjustified.

"Even if [the military orders] were permissible military procedures, I deny that it follows that they are constitutional."

Dissenting Opinion: Military Necessity Does Not Make an Order Constitutional

Robert H. Jackson

Robert H. Jackson was a justice of the Supreme Court from 1941 to 1951. Previously, he was United States attorney general. In 1945 he took a leave of absence from the Court to be the chief counsel for the prosecution of Nazi war criminals in the Nuremberg Trials. In the following dissenting opinion in Korematsu v. United States, *he argues that Japanese Americans were excluded from the West Coast only because of their ancestry and that this would be unconstitutional if it were a law. It was done not by law but under a military order, which cannot be made to conform to the Constitution, but, he maintains, the Constitution should not be distorted to approve anything that the military deems expedient, and a ruling to sustain this order would do more harm to liberty than the order itself because it would outlast the military emergency by setting legal precedent.*

[F]red] Korematsu was born on our soil, of parents born in Japan. The Constitution makes him a citizen of the United States by nativity, and a citizen of California by residence. No claim is made that he is not loyal to this country. There is no suggestion that, apart from the matter involved

Robert H. Jackson, dissenting opinion, *Korematsu v. United States*, United States Supreme Court, December 18, 1944. Reproduced by permission.

here, he is not law-abiding and well disposed. Korematsu, however, has been convicted of an act not commonly a crime. It consists merely of being present in the state whereof he is a citizen, near the place where he was born, and where all his life he has lived.

Even more unusual is the series of military orders which made this conduct a crime. They forbid such a one to remain, and they also forbid him to leave. They were so drawn that the only way Korematsu could avoid violation was to give himself up to the military authority. This meant submission to custody, examination, and transportation out of the territory, to be followed by indeterminate confinement in detention camps.

A citizen's presence in the locality, however, was made a crime only if his parents were of Japanese birth. Had Korematsu been one of four—the others being, say, a German alien enemy, an Italian alien enemy, and a citizen of American-born ancestors, convicted of treason but out on parole—only Korematsu's presence would have violated the order. The difference between their innocence and his crime would result, not from anything he did, said, or thought, different than they, but only in that he was born of different racial stock.

Now, if any fundamental assumption underlies our system, it is that guilt is personal and not inheritable. Even if all of one's antecedents had been convicted of treason, the Constitution forbids its penalties to be visited upon him, for it provides that "no attainder of treason shall work corruption of blood, or forfeiture except during the life of the person attainted." But here is an attempt to make an otherwise innocent act a crime merely because this prisoner is the son of parents as to whom he had no choice, and belongs to a race from which there is no way to resign. If Congress, in peacetime legislation, should enact such a criminal law, I should suppose this Court would refuse to enforce it.

Military Orders Differ from Laws

But the "law" which this prisoner is convicted of disregarding is not found in an act of Congress, but in a military order. Neither the Act of Congress nor the Executive Order of the President, nor both together, would afford a basis for this conviction. It rests on the orders of General [John] DeWitt. And it is said that, if the military commander had reasonable military grounds for promulgating the orders, they are constitutional, and become law, and the Court is required to enforce them. There are several reasons why I cannot subscribe to this doctrine.

It would be impracticable and dangerous idealism to expect or insist that each specific military command in an area of probable operations will conform to conventional tests of constitutionality. When an area is so beset that it must be put under military control at all, the paramount consideration is that its measures be successful, rather than legal. The armed services must protect a society, not merely its Constitution. The very essence of the military job is to marshal physical force, to remove every obstacle to its effectiveness, to give it every strategic advantage. Defense measures will not, and often should not, be held within the limits that bind civil authority in peace. No court can require such a commander in such circumstances to act as a reasonable man; he may be unreasonably cautious and exacting. Perhaps he should be. But a commander, in temporarily focusing the life of a community on defense, is carrying out a military program; he is not making law in the sense the courts know the term. He issues orders, and they may have a certain authority as military commands, although they may be very bad as constitutional law.

But if we cannot confine military expedients by the Constitution, neither would I distort the Constitution to approve all that the military may deem expedient. That is what the Court appears to be doing, whether consciously or not. I cannot say, from any evidence before me, that the orders of General DeWitt were not reasonably expedient military precautions, nor could I say that they were. But even if they were permissible military procedures, I deny that it follows that they are constitutional. If, as the Court holds, it does follow, then we may as well say that any military order will be constitutional, and have done with it.

The limitation under which courts always will labor in examining the necessity for a military order are illustrated by this case. How does the Court know that these orders have a reasonable basis in necessity? No evidence whatever on that subject has been taken by this or any other court. There is sharp controversy as to the credibility of the DeWitt report. So the Court, having no real evidence before it, has no choice but to accept General DeWitt's own unsworn, self-serving statement, untested by any cross-examination, that what he did was reasonable. And thus it will always be when courts try to look into the reasonableness of a military order.

In the very nature of things, military decisions are not susceptible of intelligent judicial appraisal. They do not pretend to rest on evidence, but are made on information that often would not be admissible and on assumptions that could not be proved. Information in support of an order could not be disclosed to courts without danger that it would reach the enemy. Neither can courts act on communications made in confidence. Hence, courts can never have any real alternative to accepting the mere declaration of the authority that issued the order that it was reasonably necessary from a military viewpoint.

Courts Should Not Rule on Military Orders

Much is said of the danger to liberty from the Army program for deporting and detaining these citizens of Japanese extraction. But a judicial construction of the due process clause that will sustain this order is a far more subtle blow to liberty than the promulgation of the order itself. A military order, however unconstitutional, is not apt to last longer than the military emergency. Even during that period, a succeeding commander may revoke it all. But once a judicial opinion rationalizes such an order to show that it conforms to the Constitution, or rather rationalizes the Constitution to show that the Constitution sanctions such an order, the Court for all time has validated the principle of racial discrimination in criminal procedure and of transplanting American citizens. The principle then lies about like a loaded weapon, ready for the hand of any authority that can bring forward a plausible claim of an urgent need. Every repetition imbeds that principle more deeply in our law and thinking and expands it to new purposes. All who observe the work of courts are familiar with what Judge [Benjamin] Cardozo described as "the tendency of a principle to expand itself to the limit of its logic." A military commander may overstep the bounds of constitutionality, and it is an incident. But if we review and approve, that passing incident becomes the doctrine of the Constitution. There it has a generative power of its own, and all that it creates will be in its own image. Nothing better illustrates this danger than does the Court's opinion in this case.

It argues that we are bound to uphold the conviction of Korematsu because we upheld one in *Hirabayashi v. United States*, when we sustained these orders insofar as they applied a curfew requirement to a citizen of Japanese ancestry. I think we should learn something from that experience.

In that case, we were urged to consider only the curfew feature, that being all that technically was involved, because it was the only count necessary to sustain Hirabayashi's conviction and sentence. We yielded, and the Chief Justice guarded the opinion as carefully as language will do. He said:

> Our investigation here does not go beyond the inquiry whether, in the light of all the relevant circumstances preceding and attending their promulgation, the challenged orders and statute *afforded a reasonable basis for the action*

taken in imposing the curfew. . . . We decide only the issue as we have defined it—we decide only that the *curfew order,* as applied, and at the time it was applied, was within the boundaries of the war power.

And again: "It is unnecessary to consider whether or to what extent *such findings would support orders differing from the curfew order.*" (Italics supplied.) However, in spite of our limiting words, we did validate a discrimination on the basis of ancestry for mild and temporary deprivation of liberty. Now the principle of racial discrimination is pushed from support of mild measures to very harsh ones, and from temporary deprivations to indeterminate ones. And the precedent which it is said requires us to do so is *Hirabayashi*. The Court is now saying that, in *Hirabayashi*, we did decide the very things we there said we were not deciding. Because we said that these citizens could be made to stay in their homes during the hours of dark, it is said we must require them to leave home entirely, and if that, we are told they may also be taken into custody for deportation, and, if that, it is argued, they may also be held for some undetermined time in detention camps. How far the principle of this case would be extended before plausible reasons would play out, I do not know.

I should hold that a civil court cannot be made to enforce an order which violates constitutional limitations even if it is a reasonable exercise of military authority. The courts can exercise only the judicial power, can apply only law, and must abide by the Constitution, or they cease to be civil courts and become instruments of military policy.

Of course, the existence of a military power resting on force, so vagrant, so centralized, so necessarily heedless of the individual, is an inherent threat to liberty. But I would not lead people to rely on this Court for a review that seems to me wholly delusive. The military reasonableness of these orders can only be determined by military superiors. If the people ever let command of the war power fall into irresponsible and unscrupulous hands, the courts wield no power equal to its restraint. The chief restraint upon those who command the physical forces of the country, in the future as in the past, must be their responsibility to the political judgments of their contemporaries and to the moral judgments of history.

My duties as a justice, as I see them, do not require me to make a military judgment as to whether General DeWitt's evacuation and detention program was a reasonable military necessity. I do not suggest that the courts should have attempted to interfere with the Army in carrying out its task. But I do not think they may be asked to execute a military expedient that has no place in law under the Constitution. I would reverse the judgment and discharge the prisoner.

| "*The evacuation orders were transparently racist.*"

The Relocation of Japanese Americans Was Motivated by Racism

Gary Kamiya

Gary Kamiya is the executive editor and one of the founders of the online magazine Salon. *In the following viewpoint he tells the story of Fred Korematsu, who resisted the order that Japanese Americans must leave the West Coast during World War II and whose case was eventually taken to the Supreme Court. Kamiya argues that the Court had no evidence that the relocation was a military necessity and that Justice Hugo Black, who wrote the Supreme Court majority opinion, was himself a racist. He then describes the discovery long after the war that government attorneys had withheld information from the Supreme Court and the subsequent reopening of Korematsu's case, after which his conviction was overturned.*

On Monday [June 28, 2004], the U.S. Supreme Court ruled that "enemy combatants"—prisoners seized in the "war on terror" whom the [George W.] Bush administration argued had no legal recourse—have the right to challenge their detention in American courts. Writing for the majority, Justice Sandra Day O'Connor wrote, "A state of war is not a blank check for the President when it comes to the rights of the Nation's citizens."

Somewhere in the San Francisco Bay Area, a soft-spoken man named Fred Korematsu is smiling.

Americans assume that their civil rights are sacrosanct, that civic tradition and the Constitution are a sure bulwark against the state's power to treat them without due process. They're wrong. Civil rights are only as strong as the nation's commitment to defending them. And the grim truth is that during wartime, that commitment often fails—especially when the gasoline of racism is poured onto the flames of fear.

That is true today, as the dark-skinned prisoners in Guantánamo and the thousands of harmless Arabs and Muslims deported or harassed after 9/11 can attest. And it was true in 1942, when Fred Korematsu, along with 120,000 other law-abiding Americans of Japanese ancestry—two-thirds of them American citizens—were forcibly removed from their homes, farms, businesses and communities and sent into imprisonment in desolate camps throughout the West. Their crime? Being of Japanese descent. It was the greatest mass violation of civil rights in 20th century American history.

Fred Korematsu resisted the order. He took his case to the Supreme Court. Of the four Supreme Court cases brought by Japanese-Americans involving the internment order, his was the only one in which the court directly ruled on the constitutionality of the relocation order. In what is now regarded as one of the most disgraceful rulings in the court's history, he lost—and to this day, the right of the government to act as it did in 1942 has never been overturned. But his defeat carried within it the seeds of a larger victory. Forty-one years later, a legal team made up of mostly young Japanese-American lawyers—many of whose parents had been in the camps—brought suit to bring justice not just to Korematsu, but also to all those who had been wronged by the internment orders. In a stunned and tearful California courtroom, his conviction for refusing to report to an "assembly center" was overturned, and the shame of a dark moment in American history was finally washed away.

Five years later, President Bill Clinton awarded Korematsu the nation's highest civilian award, the Presidential Medal of Freedom. That award recognized that the unassuming young welder had stood up for something larger than himself. Fred Korematsu, who would not go into the camps, had joined [black civil rights activist] Rosa Parks, who would not give up her seat [on a segregated bus], in the most exclusive, yet most universal, American club: the club of ordinary heroes.

"We should be vigilant to make sure this will never happen again," Korematsu said upon receiving the Medal of Freedom. And he has practiced that vigilance himself. Last October [2003], he joined a friend-of-the-court [amicus curiae] brief to the Supreme Court, arguing that the extended executive detentions of "enemy combatants" are unconstitutional. Few amicus petitioners have carried more moral authority.

Fred Korematsu's Arrest

The event that was to change Fred Korematsu's life forever took place on Feb. 19, 1942, a little more than two months after Pearl Harbor. That was the day that President Franklin Delano Roosevelt—acting under pressure from military authorities, the media and West Coast political leaders—signed Executive Order 9066, authorizing the mass evacuation of 120,000 Americans of Japanese ancestry from the West Coast. The reason given was that the Japanese constituted a military threat. No evidence was ever presented for this claim. Roosevelt did not discuss the order with his cabinet, nor did he ask for justification.

Among the thousands of those affected was the Korematsu family, which ran a nursery in Oakland. The elder Korematsus, like almost all other Americans of Japanese descent, planned to obey without protest. But their son, 22-year-old Fred Korematsu, took a different view. He thought it was wrong and unfair that he should be forced to abandon his home and be sent to a far-off prison camp simply because of his race. After talking things over with his parents and his Italian-American girlfriend, he decided not to go. He was one of only a handful of Japanese-Americans who refused to comply with the internment order.

Korematsu, who had been working as a welder in a shipyard, changed his name and had minor plastic surgery to make himself look less Japanese. He succeeded in avoiding the authorities for about three months, but on May 30, 1942, someone recognized him in a San Leandro store and called police. He was arrested and sent to Tanforan Race Track, where Japanese-Americans were processed (sleeping in horse stalls reeking of manure) before being shipped off to various desolate camps on the wind-swept plateaus of the West. Korematsu was sent to the internment camp at Topaz, Utah.

Before he departed, however, he was visited in jail by a man named Ernest Besig, the executive director of the Northern California chapter of the American Civil Liberties Union. He had read about Korematsu in the paper. He had been looking for a Japanese-American who would challenge the legality of the internment order—a test case. Besig was acting without institutional sanction: the national ACLU, intimidated by war fervor, had decided not to challenge the constitutionality of the internment. He asked the young man if he would agree to go to court.

Korematsu was utterly alone. His family was already gone. His girlfriend was, too—in fact, he never saw her again. His community was scattered. The conservative Japanese American Citizens League, the sole group representing both Issei (Japan-born Americans, forbidden by racist U.S. law from becoming citizens) and Nisei (their American-born children) had decided for strategic reasons to go along quietly with whatever the authorities ordered. By fighting the government, Korematsu risked alienating himself from his peers, many of whom had decided that the only way to prove their loyalty was to keep their heads down.

Racist Attitudes

Korematsu agreed to fight the government in court. In October 1944, with World War II heading into its brutal final winter, Korematsu's case reached the Supreme Court. The government's lawyers argued that in wartime, the military was required to take all steps necessary to protect the national security. It cited a report by General [John] DeWitt, the officer responsible for the defense of the West Coast (and whose recommendation was responsible for Executive Order 9066), claiming that many people of Japanese ancestry were disloyal and that there was no time to figure out which of them were loyal and which were not.

Korematsu's lawyers charged that the evacuation orders were transparently racist and denied an entire class of people due process and equal protection under the law. They pointed out that not a single episode of espionage or sabotage had taken place during the four months between Pearl Harbor and General DeWitt's first evacuation order. . . . They argued that DeWitt was himself a racist, citing this statement he made in 1943 before a congressional committee: "A Jap's a Jap. It makes no difference whether he is an American citizen or not. I don't want any of them . . . They are a dangerous element, whether loyal or not."

DeWitt's viewpoint was probably shared in some form by most Americans. At bottom, the fear was of a racially tinged "clash of civilizations": the Japanese were mysterious and opaque, not "real" Americans, and when the chips were down they were likely to betray their new nation in favor of their race. This belief was eloquently expressed by none other than Earl Warren, the California attorney general who was later to become the famously liberal chief justice of the United States. Testifying in 1942 before a House committee. Warren said, "the consensus of opinion among the law-enforcement officers of this State is that there is more potential danger among the group of Japanese who are born in this country than from the alien Japanese who were born in Japan. We believe that when we are dealing with the Caucasian race we have methods that will test the loyalty of them, and we believe that we can, in dealing with the Germans and Italians, arrive at some fairly sound conclusions because of our knowledge of the way they live in the community and have lived for many years. But when we deal with the Japanese we are in an entirely different field and we can not form any opinion that we believe to be sound."

This, then, was the intellectual climate in which the Supreme Court heard the case. On Dec. 18, 1944, the court handed down its decision. The divided court (6-3) ruled against Korematsu. In his majority opinion, Justice Hugo Black essentially deferred to the military authorities and Congress, who had stated that the presence of an uncertain number of disloyal Japanese made it necessary to remove all of them from the coast. . . .

Black denied that racism lay behind the relocation order, only military necessity. But neither he nor the rest of the majority seemed interested in trying to find out just what that military necessity was. Certainly little evidence, and no convincing evidence, was advanced of Japanese-American disloyalty. (In fact, not a single case of sabotage or espionage by Japanese-Americans ever took place during the entire war.) Black cited the fact that 5,000 internees refused to swear unqualified allegiance to the United States, overlooking the fact that their forcible removal from their homes and businesses without legal recourse might have had something to do with their refusal. Nor did he deal with the uncomfortable fact that neither Italian-Americans nor German-Americans were evacuated from their homes and forced into prison camps.

It is difficult to escape the conclusion that Black, who was a former member of the Ku Klux Klan, subscribed at some level to the same racist beliefs that infected so many other

Americans. Why else would he have so uncritically accepted the feeble national-security arguments advanced by the government?

Whatever his motivations, it was a decision that was reportedly to haunt Black for the rest of his life. After all, Black was one of the court's greatest defenders of civil liberties, author of the now-classic decision in the landmark Pentagon Papers case. (Ironically, the most towering civil liberties advocate in court history, Justice William O. Douglas, concurred with the majority in Korematsu.) But though troubled by the ruling, Black was never able to bring himself to admit he was wrong. In a 1967 interview, Black said, "I would do precisely the same thing today, in any part of the country. I would probably issue the same order were I President. We had a situation where we were at war. People were rightly fearful of the Japanese in Los Angeles, many loyal to the United States, many undoubtedly not, having dual citizenship—lots of them. They all look alike to a person not a Jap. Had they [the Japanese] attacked our shores you'd have a large number fighting with the Japanese troops. And a lot of innocent Japanese-Americans would have been shot in the panic. Under these circumstances I saw nothing wrong in moving them away from the danger area."

In a biting dissent, Justice Frank Murphy called the ruling "a legalization of racism." But Korematsu had lost.

The Case Reopened

The war ended and Korematsu, along with thousands of other internees, got out of the camps and on with his life. He did not like to talk about his Supreme Court case; in fact, his own daughter only learned about it in class. He wanted to reopen his case but didn't know how. It was not until 1983 that his now-ancient legal battle stirred again. . . .

A San Diego historian and law professor named Peter Irons made the kind of discovery that historians, lawyers and journalists can only dream about: He came upon documentary evidence proving that the government had knowingly lied to the Supreme Court in the original Korematsu case. . . .

The documents showed that the solicitor-general of the United States, Charles Fahey, knew that all of the military's arguments that Japanese-Americans were engaging in subversive behavior were contradicted by reports from the FBI and military intelligence—and failed to share that information with the court. Smoking guns don't get much more billowing.

Irons visited Korematsu at his San Leandro home and showed him the documents. Korematsu sat in silence for 15 or 20 minutes, puffing on his pipe, reading the documents. Then he asked Irons, "Are you a lawyer?" Irons said he was. "Would you be my lawyer?"

And so the battle was joined again. This time, Korematsu would win.

A legal team led by Irons and a young Sansei (third-generation Japanese-American) lawyer named Dale Minami filed a coram nobis petition on Korematsu's behalf in a San Francisco district court. "Coram nobis" is Latin for "before us": Like the related writ of habeas corpus, which protects against illegal detention, coram nobis applies to those individuals who have been convicted wrongfully and have served their sentence. To prove coram nobis, the petitioner must show that a fundamental error or manifest injustice has been committed. Only egregious errors of fact or prosecutorial misconduct, not interpretations of the law, will result in a successful coram nobis writ.

Fortunately, that is exactly what Korematsu's attorneys had. In fact, so incendiary were the documents that the lawyers feared they would "disappear"; they met in secret for many months. The team made a tactical decision to file in the District Court, rather than to the high court, because there was a much greater chance they would lose in the Supreme Court.

The government, clearly aware that it was doomed, stalled, arguing about procedure. It offered Korematsu a pardon—which of course implies guilt. Korematsu refused.

Finally the judge hearing the case, Marilyn Hall Patel, grew impatient with the government's delaying tactics. . . . She prepared a substantive decision to read in the courtroom the next day, knowing that it would be packed with people.

The next day, the government made its arguments. It argued that the case should not be reopened because to do so would be to reopen old wounds. There was no reason to go back and try to find out what actually happened back then, the government said—why not just let bygones be bygones?

Minami responded by pointing out that the only "old wounds" that would be reopened would be those of a government that had lied to the Supreme Court, not those of people who had already lost their homes and livelihood. Then he asked if Fred Korematsu could make a short statement.

Korematsu said that 41 years ago, he entered this courtroom in handcuffs and was sent to a camp that was not fit for human habitation. Horse stalls are for horses, not people. He asked the court to overturn his conviction, saying, in Minami's recollection, "that what happened to him could happen to any American citizen who looks different or who comes from a different country and that it was important for this court to understand that the relief given to him was not just for him personally, but in a sense, for the benefit of the whole country."

Victory at Last

When Korematsu finished, Patel read her ruling to the courtroom right from the bench. She said that there was sufficient evidence of governmental misconduct to overturn the conviction. Evidence had been suppressed. The policies of the U.S. government were infected with racism. She said that the Constitution had to be protected at all times for all people. Then she got up and left the court.

For a moment, after she left, the entire audience was stunned. History had been made in front of their eyes: a great injustice had been legally expunged. But it was too big to take in. Korematsu asked someone, "What happened?" He was told, "You won." Then it sank in. The crowd, many of them camp survivors, was overcome with emotion. They swarmed Korematsu, hugged him. Tears flowed—but this time they were tears of vindication. The young shipyard welder's long odyssey had finally ended. He had carried not just himself, but also his people, into the safe harbor of belated justice. That justice did not make up for lives shattered, property lost, hopes blighted. But it helped.

Korematsu's victory was not complete. The Supreme Court ruling in his case has never been overturned; it remains on the books, like a malignant virus, waiting to be activated when racist paranoia and war hysteria sweep aside Americans' commitment to civil rights. Every generation seems condemned to fight the same battles on different grounds: Guantánamo is today's Heart Mountain [a relocation center where Japanese Americans were sent]. But the knowledge that ordinary people like Fred Korematsu are there, willing to stand quietly up for their rights, makes it possible to dream that one day the battle will be won.

"Experience during the war did demonstrate that there were a sizeable number of Japanese-Americans who militantly supported Japan."

The Relocation of Japanese Americans Was a Response to a Real Danger

Dwight D. Murphey

Dwight D. Murphey, a retired law professor, is the author of many books and articles. In the following excerpt from a long article about the relocation of the Japanese Americans during World War II, he argues that they were not imprisoned but merely barred from the West Coast, that conditions in the relocation camps were much better than they have been portrayed by critics, and that although the vast majority of Japanese Americans were loyal citizens, there were some who supported and even spied for Japan.

In my opinion, the United States did *not* act shamefully in its treatment of persons of Japanese ancestry during World War II. In fact, a better case could be made for a diametrically opposite criticism: that the treatment was so tender-hearted that it actually endangered the security of the United States during a desperate war.

In the intolerant context of today's ideological arguments, it is predictable that a conclusion favorable to the United States will be represented as "offensive" to the many splendid

Dwight D. Murphey, "The Relocation of the Japanese Americans During World War II," dwightmurphy-collectedwritings.info/published/pub38.htm, 1995. Reproduced by permission of the author. The entire article can be found at http://www.dwight murphy-collectedwritings.info/published/pub38.

people of Japanese ancestry who now form a part of the American people. But that, of course, is nonsense. The search for historical accuracy isn't a panderer's game to curry favor. To seek the truth is no slander against anyone. . . .

West Coast Declared a Military Zone

On February 19, 1942, President Franklin D. Roosevelt signed Executive Order 9066. This authorized the establishment of military areas from which people of all kinds could be excluded. Lt. General John L. DeWitt was appointed the military commander to carry out the Executive Order. In March, Gen. DeWitt declared large parts of the Pacific Coast states military areas in which no one of Japanese descent would be allowed to remain. The exclusion order affected Japanese-Americans living on the West Coast by forcing them to move inland. Its only effect upon those who already lived inland was to bar them from going to the quarantined areas on the West Coast. . . .

There was a continuing tension, lessening over time, between the desire to let the evacuees relocate freely and the public's desire to have them closely monitored.

This led to the "assembly center phase," during which the evacuees were moved to improvised centers such as race tracks and fairgrounds along the West Coast pending the construction of ten "relocation centers" in eastern California, Arizona, Utah, Idaho, Wyoming, Colorado, and as far east as Arkansas. During this phase, federal officials made extensive efforts to lessen public hostility. As those feelings subsided, approximately 4,000 families moved inland "on their own recognizance" to communities of their choice before the assembly center phase was over at the end of the summer of 1942. [Karl R.] Bendetsen [who was named director of the Wartime Civil Control Administration and handled the evacuation] says that all of the Japanese-Americans could have moved on their own at any time if they had seen their way clear to do it. . . .

Hastily improvised and purely temporary quarters for thousands of people who have been uprooted from their homes on short notice could not have been pleasant. There is no incongruity, however, between this and the fact, also true, that the government worked with the evacuees to take extraordinary measures to make the centers as comfortable as possible. In the short time they existed, some centers opened libraries; movies were shown regularly; there were Scout troops, arts and crafts classes, musical groups, and leagues for basketball and baseball. Three hundred and fifty people signed up for a calisthenics class at Stockton. All had playgrounds for children, and one even had a pitch-and-putt golf course. The centers were run almost entirely by the Japanese-Americans themselves.

As the ten relocation centers became ready, the evacuees were moved to them from the assembly centers. . . . The construction of the camps was of the type used for housing American soldiers overseas—which is to say, the centers were austere but functional. . . . It is worth noting that no families were ever separated during the process. . . .

There were messhalls for meals, and a large number of community enterprises, which included stores, theaters, hairdressers, community theaters, and newspapers. There was ping-pong, judo, boxing, badminton, and sumo wrestling. Again, there were basketball and baseball leagues (along with some touch football). The Santa Fe center had [according to the testimony of assistant secretary of war John J. McCloy] "gardens, two softball diamonds, two tennis courts, a miniature nine-hole golf course, a fenced forty-acre hiking area, . . . classes in calligraphy, Chinese and Japanese poetry. . . ." The Massachusetts Quakers sponsored art competitions. Libraries featured Japanese-language sections. There were chapters of the American Red Cross, YMCA, YWCA, Boy Scouts, and Girl Scouts. State Shinto, with its emperor-worship, was barred, but otherwise the evacuees worshipped as they pleased. The government paid a salary equal to an American soldier's pay ($21 per month) to those who worked in the centers. . . .

Even before the relocation centers became filled, college-age students began to leave to attend American universities. By the beginning of the fall semester in 1942, approximately 250 students had left for school, attending 143 colleges and universities. By the time the war was over, 4,300 college-age students were attending more than 300 universities around the country (though not on the West Coast). Scholarships were granted based on financial ability. Foundations and churches funded a "National Japanese American Student Relocation Council" to help with college attendance.

The centers were intended, as their name suggests, to be places in which the evacuees could stay while they were being relocated around the country. [U.S. senator] S. I. Hayakawa tells us, "hundreds of Issei [foreign-born Japanese American] railroad workers were restored to their jobs in eastern Oregon." At one point, $4 million was appropriated to help those who wanted to start businesses away from the centers. In 1943, 16,000 people left the centers on indefinite leave; and 18,500 more followed in 1944. . . .

Many of the evacuees, however, remained in the centers for the duration of the war. Critics attribute this to a lack of alternatives, as though the evacuees were trapped, but Bendetsen credits the fact that life was acceptable within the centers. "Many elected to stay in the relocation centers while being gainfully employed in nearby pursuits in the general economy . . . The climate of hostility which presented intractable problems in the very early phases had long since subsided."

Relocation or Internment?

There is no question but that the evacuees were forced by law to leave their homes on the West Coast and to either stay in the centers or relocate elsewhere in the United States by receiving leaves for the purpose. Their exclusion from the West

Coast was not voluntary, and after the short-lived initial phase their relocation had to be done through the centers, which granted leave, temporary or indefinite, for the purpose. But, except for those arrested as 'dangerous aliens' right after Pearl Harbor and those who were later segregated at Tule Lake, were the Japanese-Americans "interned" in the centers? And were the centers, as is often charged, "concentration camps"? . . .

The substance of the charge of "internment" is contradicted by the fact that resettlement outside the centers was diligently pursued throughout the process. Hayakawa says that by January 2, 1945, half of those evacuated had "found new jobs and homes in mid-America and the East."

What is most often pointed to in support of the charge of "internment" and even of the centers' being "concentration camps" is that there were "fences and guards." Even Hayakawa speaks of the centers as being "behind barbed wire, guarded by armed sentries." Oddly, however, the role of fences and guards depends largely upon perception.

In 1984 a House subcommittee asked Bendetsen about earlier testimony that there had been barbed wire and watchtowers, and he testified that "that is 100 percent false . . . Because of the actions of outraged U.S. citizens, of which I do not approve, it was necessary in some of the assembly centers, particularly Santa Anita, . . . to protect the evacuees . . . and that is the only place where guards were used." . . .

There were strong reasons for an actual internment, which is what Earl Warren, then the attorney general of California, wanted. But that is not what the Roosevelt administration did. It chose to steer a middle course between those who wanted no evacuation at all and those who, like Warren, wanted the Japanese-American population closely monitored. To call it an "internment" is at most a half-truth. . . .

Economic Losses and Property Care

Unscrupulous people took advantage of the situation in which the Japanese-Americans found themselves between the time of Pearl Harbor on December 7, 1941, and early March of the following year. But once the Army took charge of the evacuation, extensive efforts were made to safeguard the evacuees' property. Col. Bendetsen testified:

> When you are told that the household goods of the evacuees after I took over were dissipated, that is totally false. The truth is that all of the household goods of those who were evacuated or who left voluntarily were indexed, stored, and warehouse receipts were given. And those who settled in the interior on their own told us, and we shipped it to them free of charge. As far as their crops were concerned, the allegations are totally false. I used the Agriculture Department to arrange harvesting after they left and to sell the crops at auction, and the Federal Reserve System, at my request, handled the proceeds. The proceeds were carefully deposited in their bank accounts in the West to each individual owner. And many of these farms were farmed the whole time—not sold at bargain prices, but leased—and the proceeds were based the market value of the harvest.

As we will see, Congress passed a "Claims Act" in 1948 under which approximately $38 million was paid to the evacuees for property losses. The critics assert that additional compensation should have been granted for mental suffering, but that is a different issue than whether there was a wanton taking of their property. Many millions of people, including Americans of all origins and by no means limited to the Japanese-Americans, experienced uncompensated mental suffering in World War II. . . .

West Coast Vulnerability Was Real

The critics of the evacuation often argue that there was no demonstrated military necessity for it. The Report of the Commission on Wartime Relocation speaks of "the clamor" by California officials for protective action, and says that "these opinions were not informed by any knowledge of actual military risks." The extensive critical literature mocks the perception of danger, suggesting that it was a figment of hysterical imaginations.

But this is nonsense. The danger was apparent to anyone who considered the situation. Earl Warren, as attorney general of California, testified before a select committee of Congress on February 21, 1942, and submitted letters from a number of local officials. Some pointed to the vulnerability of the water supply and of the large-scale irrigation systems: . . . Another pointed out that "a systematic campaign of incendiarism would cause terrific disaster" during the California dry season from May until October. The city manager of Alameda observed that "we have the naval air station at one end of the island . . . There are five major shipyards along the northern edge and there is the Oakland Airport at the eastern end of the island." . . .

In addition to the civilian population, there was much that was important militarily and economically along the West Coast; it was clearly exposed; and there were few means to defend it. This was enough in itself to create a critical emergency, to be met as humanely but as effectively as possible. It should not be necessary for the American government to have known specifically of plans for espionage and sabotage.

Just the same, there *was* definitive evidence of Japan's intent to exploit (and actual exploitation of) the situation. On December 4, 1941, the Office of Naval Intelligence reported a Japanese "intelligence machine geared for war, in operation, and utilizing west coast Japanese." On January 21, 1942, a bulletin from Army Intelligence "stated flat out that the Japanese government's espionage net containing Japanese aliens, first and second generation Japanese and other nationals is now thoroughly organized and working underground," according to the testimony of David D. Lowman, a retired career intelligence officer who has written extensively on declassified intelligence from World War II.

The Commission on Wartime Relocation contradicted this in its 1982 Report when it said that "not a single documented act of espionage, sabotage or fifth column activity was committed by an American citizen of Japanese ancestry or by a resident Japanese alien on the West Coast." This claim is often repeated in the critical literature, but is blatantly false.

Evidence from Japanese Dispatches

Amazingly, the Commission ignored the most important source of information about espionage, which is the dispatches sent by the Japanese government to its own officials before and during the war. U.S. Navy codebreakers had broken the Japanese diplomatic code in 1938, and the decoded messages were distributed, on a basis "higher than Top Secret," to a small handful of the very highest American officials under the codename "MAGIC." Lowman testified in 1984 that "included among the diplomatic communications were hundreds of reports dealing with espionage activities in the United States and its possessions . . . In recruiting Japanese second generation and resident nationals, Tokyo warned to use the utmost caution . . . In April [1941], Tokyo instructed all the consulates to wire home lists of first- and second-generation Japanese according to specified categories." The result, he said, was that "in May 1941, Japanese consulates on the west coast reported to Tokyo that first and second generation Japanese had been successfully recruited and were now spying on shipments of airplanes and war material in the San Diego and San Pedro areas. They were reporting on activities within aircraft plants in Seattle and Los Angeles. Local Japanese . . . were reporting on shipping activities at the Bremerton Naval Yard . . . The Los Angeles consulate reported: 'We shall maintain connections with our second generation who are at present in the Army to keep us informed' . . . Seattle followed with a similar dispatch."

Several officials within the Roosevelt administration opposed the evacuation of the Japanese-Americans from the West Coast, but Lowman makes a telling point: that the President, the Secretary of War, the Army Chief of Staff, the Director of Military Intelligence, the Secretary of the Navy, the Chief of Naval Operations, the Director of Naval Intelligence, and the Chiefs of Army and Navy Plans—all of whom received MAGIC—*favored* evacuation. It was those who did not have knowledge of the Japanese dispatches who found it possible, somewhat incongruously in light of the self-evident factors I have mentioned, to doubt the military necessity. . . .

Japanese Americans Not Assimilated

The nature of the Japanese-American community on the West Coast at the time of World War II posed a dual problem. Because it was tightly-knit and unassimilated, it was attractive to Japan as a field for cultivation. At the same time, it was virtually impenetrable to efforts of the American government to sort out those whose loyalties were with Japan.

On the Supreme Court, Justice [Harlan] Stone wrote that "there is support for the view that social, economic and political conditions which have prevailed since the close of the last century . . . have intensified their solidarity and have in large measure prevented their assimilation." Stone estimated that as many as 10,000 of those born in the United States had "been sent to Japan for all or part of their education." He observed that even those who stayed in the United States to go to school "are sent to Japanese language schools outside the regular hours of public schools in the locality." S.I. Hayakawa wrote that it was true that "reverence for the emperor was taught in the Japanese-language schools." . . .

It is important to note again that it is no reflection on today's Americans of Japanese ancestry to take an honest look at what the situation was fifty years ago during World War II.

Many did strongly identify with the American side, and even distinguished themselves in combat on behalf of this country. An all-Nisei [second-generation Japanese Americans] National Guard unit from Hawaii, the 100th Battalion, fought in Italy, winning much distinction, and was later merged into a newly-formed group, the 442nd Combat Team, which went on to fight in both Italy and France. In all, close to 9,000 Japanese-Americans served with these units. They were honored by President [Harry] Truman in 1946 after a parade down Constitution Avenue [in Washington, D.C.], and in turn raised money for a memorial to President Roosevelt. An additional 3,700 Nisei served as translators and interpreters in the Pacific Theater. In all, out of the combined mainland and Hawaiian Japanese-American populations, a total of more than 33,000 are said to have served in some capacity during the war.

To focus exclusively on this, however, obscures the truth, which taken as a whole was much more complex. . . .

A significant number [of evacuees] sought repatriation to Japan. 9,028 applications were filed by the end of 1943, a total that swelled to 19,014 by a year later. Eventually, more than 16 percent of the evacuees asked for repatriation. Of these, 8,000 actually went back to Japan. . . .

There was a powerful pro-Japan element within the relocation centers, forcing its members' eventual segregation into the facility at Tule Lake. Secretary of War Henry L. Stimson wrote in May 1943 about "a vicious, well-organized, pro-Japanese group to be found at each relocation center. Through agitation and violence, these groups gained control of many aspects of internal project administration, so much so that it became disadvantageous, and sometimes dangerous, to express loyalty to the United States." . . .

The militants at Tule Lake formed into two groups. John J. Culley, an author who writes as part of the critical literature, tells us that "both groups practiced nationalistic activities with military overtones, including marching and drilling, bugle calls, playing the Japanese national anthem, celebrating the eighth of each month in commemoration of the attack on Pearl Harbor, wearing short military-style haircuts, and wearing rising-sun emblems on their coats and shirts."

If Japan had invaded the West Coast, enormous pressures would have come to bear to support the invading army. Col. Bendetsen testified that wherever the Japanese invaded they shot those of Japanese ancestry who did not embrace them—and that this fact was well known. . . .

A Dangerously Indulgent Policy?

Many officials on the West Coast and in the western states wanted actual internment, not just relocation, for the duration of the war. Hindsight shows that this wasn't necessary. As it turned out, the evacuation and relocation worked well to protect both the national security and the Japanese-Americans themselves.

It is easy to lose sight of the fact today, however, that the decision not to intern them was made at great risk. Experience during the war did demonstrate that there were a sizeable number of Japanese-Americans who militantly supported Japan. If they had conducted even one massive act of sabotage, would the risk have been worth it? How many lives, say, was the risk worth? 100? 1,000? 10,000? Whose lives? . . .

The normal course of law in a legal system that respects individual rights looks at the guilt of individuals, providing each "due process." The critics of the evacuation invoke this as the ground for a bitter denunciation of American policy, since the policy treated the Japanese-Americans as a group.

The critical view would follow almost naturally from a position that acknowledges virtually no need for protective measures in the emergency: If the threat were slight, it would hardly outweigh the important value to be given to individual due process. We have already seen, however, that there *was* a vital need for immediate action.

The critical view would also be reasonable if the American government had had an expeditious way to determine, by investigation and hearings, the loyalty of each person on an individual basis. But this was a virtual impossibility, given the cultural insularity of the Japanese-American community. . . .

Was Relocation a Product of Racism?

Much public opinion on the West Coast had long been hostile to Japanese and other Asian immigration. Organized labor was for many years prominent among its opponents. And there is no question but that public opinion was inflamed against the Japanese during World War II, especially immediately following Pearl Harbor. This feeling was most intense on the West Coast, for a very specific reason: the National Guard units from eleven western states were fighting in the Philippines, where they were tortured and starved by their Japanese captors. Their families and friends felt passionately about these atrocities.

Throughout the war, one of the motivating factors in the policy of evacuation and resettlement was to protect the Japanese-Americans from public anger. It is easy today to say that that anger was "racist," but we have reason to be suspicious of attitudes taken under much more comfortable circumstances forty and even fifty years after the fact. To argue that the anger was vicious has, itself, a certain vicious quality about it.

There were ample reasons for the evacuation that had nothing to do with racism. Justice [Hugo] Black wrote level-headedly about this in 1944: "To cast this case into outlines of racial prejudice, without reference to the real military dangers which were present, merely confuses the issue. Korematsu was not excluded from the Military Area because of hostility to him or his race . . . He *was* excluded because we are at war with the Japanese Empire. . . ."

Justice Stone discussed whether there are occasions when national origin can be considered in making policy: "Because racial discriminations are in most circumstances irrelevant and therefore prohibited, it by no means follows that, in dealing with the perils of war, Congress and the Executive are wholly precluded from taking into account those facts and circumstances which are relevant . . . and which may in fact place citizens of one ancestry in a different category from others." . . .

The circumstances during World War II were much more complicated than those who would damn the United States as having "viciously set up concentration camps for the Japanese-Americans" ever admit. My study of the subject has persuaded me that Americans have nothing to be ashamed of about this episode, even though it is regrettable that war and its incidents ever have to happen.

"By standing up against the treacherous collusion of racism, national security and unaccountable government power, Korematsu changed this nation."

Fred Korematsu Was a Hero

Dorothy Ehrlich

Dorothy Ehrlich is the deputy executive director of the American Civil Liberties Union. In the following article written in 2005, shortly after the death of Fred Korematsu, she maintains that he was imprisoned during World War II solely because of his race. After summarizing his case and its later reopening she tells about his activism on behalf of justice for Japanese Americans in later years, the inspiration he offered to activists for similar causes, and his receipt of the Medal of Freedom from president Bill Clinton.

I did not expect to sing "America the Beautiful" along with nearly 1,000 people at a recent memorial for Fred Korematsu, a true American hero who died March 30.

It did not occur to me that this patriotic standard would be fitting for a man who defied the World War II executive order sending Japanese Americans to concentration camps. An American citizen who was vilified and imprisoned in his own country—first in prison for his defiance and later in an internment camp where he was sent without any evidence that he was a danger to this country. Fred Korematsu—like 120,000 other Americans of Japanese descent—was imprisoned solely because of his race.

Dorothy Ehrlich, "Courageous Hero Inspires America to Become More Beautiful," *The Daily Journal*, May 11, 2005. Reproduced by permission.

It must have been a painfully lonely time for Korematsu, his family and friends shipped off to places that hardly would conjure up the majesty of purple mountains. The camps were scattered throughout the western United States—from dusty Topaz, Utah, to the swamplands of Rowher, Ark.—leaving the 22-year-old welder with literally no one to call for help as the headlines blared: "Jap Spy Arrested in San Leandro."

While in jail, a stranger came to his aid. Ernest Besig, the executive director of the ACLU of Northern California, read about a young Japanese American who had been arrested by police on an East Bay street corner, handcuffed and thrown in jail. Besig visited him and offered to post bail and lend his support and legal assistance.

The ACLU of Northern California agreed to represent Korematsu in 1942, a decision that was intensely controversial inside and outside of the organization. The case, challenging the constitutionality of the executive order that allowed the military to summarily exclude Japanese Americans en masse from the West Coast and eventually imprison them, ultimately went to the U.S. Supreme Court.

The high court ruled 6-3 against Korematsu in 1944. Law students still study that infamous decision upholding the Roosevelt administration's action as necessary for wartime security, and it remains a stain upon the nation's commitment to justice.

Korematsu's courageous decision to defy Executive Order 9066, and his stinging defeat in the U.S. Supreme Court, were memories he and many other internees wanted to put behind them. It wasn't until the movement for redress emerged in the late 1970s as a politically viable issue that the Japanese American community, along with other civil rights supporters, began to question the government's World War II treatment of Japanese Americans and to shine light on the relevant lessons of that injustice.

In that new political atmosphere, law professor and historian Peter Irons, and researcher Aiko Yoshinaga Herzig, discovered hidden documents in the National Archives. These documents proved that wartime military officials not only lacked any evidence of Japanese American disloyalty, but rather, that the government deliberately concealed and destroyed evidence to the contrary in an effort to give the U.S. Supreme Court the impression that the wartime exclusion and internment were a "military necessity."

In 1982, Peter Irons shared his discovery with Korematsu and asked the former internee if he would be interested in re-opening his case. Korematsu carefully read the documents, and responded in a soft but strong voice, "They did me a great wrong." He agreed to seek vindication.

Korematsu's decision to leave his quiet suburban life, where hard work and commitment to family and community were his focus, and to re-enter the political and judicial fray around Japanese American internment motivated a team of young attorneys, many of whom were sons and daughters of internees. These creative young lawyers crafted a legal strategy using a rare legal procedure, a writ of error coram nobis to ask a federal judge to vacate Korematsu's criminal conviction for refusing to obey the internment order.

On Nov. 10, 1983, some 40 years after his imprisonment, U.S. District Judge Marilyn Hall Patel announced to a packed San Francisco courtroom that she was vacating Korematsu's conviction. In issuing her ruling, Patel acknowledged that the government's actions against Japanese Americans were based "on unsubstantiated facts, distortions and representations of at least one military commander, whose views were seriously infected by racism."

A tearful crowd, many of whom had been imprisoned in America's concentration camps during World War II, greeted Patel's decision, rendered directly from the bench, with joy and disbelief.

When Korematsu stepped out of Patel's courtroom on that autumn day, he was surrounded by reporters. He spoke in a clear and simple manner about fairness and the relief of at last being vindicated. It is a message he would deliver many times to many audiences as he criss-crossed the nation during the next 25 years. Korematsu became a powerful leader in the redress movement of the 1980s, which secured legislation, signed by President Ronald Reagan, that provided for an official governmental apology as well as symbolic financial restitution to former internees.

Korematsu taught a whole new generation about the government's misdeeds during World War II, and the impact it had on the Japanese American community. As Eva Paterson, president of the Equal Justice Society, said, "He served as a reminder that wrongs can be righted. Momentary defeat followed by ultimate triumph is what Mr. Korematsu meant to me."

Korematsu's story of courage has inspired a new generation of lawyers and activists. By standing up against the treacherous collusion of racism, national security and unaccountable government power, Korematsu changed this nation. As explained by Dale Minami, one of the lawyers who represented Korematsu in the coram nobis proceeding, Fred Korematsu was the Rosa Parks for a generation of Asian Americans.

Perhaps no single action by the government represents a greater breach of civil liberties in our nation's history than the internment of Japanese Americans during World War II. There was a period of time when we thought this could never happen again. And then came Sept. 11, 2001.

In the aftermath of 9/11, our government launched a series of actions that have violated civil liberties—holding prisoners without charges and engaging in torture at the U.S. Naval Base at Guantanamo Bay, Cuba, rounding up and questioning tens of thousands of young men based solely on their national origin, issuing no-fly lists at airports and engaging in surveillance of library records.

But for the education that has taken place over the last quarter century, the public outcry over these violations could have been greatly subdued. For in 1942, the ACLU stood virtually alone in its condemnation of the government's action. Today, scores of organizations stand shoulder-to-shoulder in fighting effectively against these abuses; nearly 400 communities in every state have passed resolutions calling for limiting the reach of the USA Patriot Act.

And last year, when the U.S. Supreme Court reviewed the issue of the government's current abuse of power at Guantanamo Bay, it had the benefit of an influential brief filed on behalf of Korematsu telling his own story in the context of this country's long history of violating civil liberties in times of national crisis.

In 1998, President Bill Clinton bestowed the Medal of Freedom, this nation's highest civilian honor, to Korematsu for his courage. The proclamation delivered by Clinton stated, "In the long history of our country's constant search for justice, some names of ordinary citizens stand for millions of souls ... Plessy, Brown, Parks. ... To that distinguished list, today we add the name of Fred Korematsu."

Korematsu's life and the lessons he taught us remind us of the fragility of civil liberties and the potential for political movements, with activists and lawyers working together, to vindicate our rights. And at the close of Korematsu's memorial, a quartet of trumpets etched his memory in our hearts as they rang out with Aaron Copland's "Fanfare for the Common Man." They reminded us that under these spacious skies, a very patriotic American once stood hopelessly alone, but the simple justice embodied in his singular act of courage eventually drew us and our nation to stand with him.

CHAPTER 2

Refusing a Stay of Execution to Cold War Spies

Case Overview

Rosenberg v. United States (1953)

In the late 1940s Americans were stunned by the reality of the atomic bomb, the weapon that had ended World War II yet created the potential for even worse wars that might come in the future. In particular, they were increasingly disturbed by worry about the long-term intentions of the Soviet Union, which had been an ally during the war but was rapidly developing into a dangerous opponent. Information about the bomb during its development had not been shared with the Soviets, but by 1949, to America's surprise and dismay, the Soviets had begun testing their own atomic weapons. It was believed that they could not have progressed so fast without access to secret information, and the fact that spies had indeed passed such information to them was soon discovered.

Among those arrested was David Greenglass, who accused his sister Ethel's husband, Julius Rosenberg, of involvement. It was eventually determined that Julius and Ethel had been running a spy ring since the last years of the war. There was little evidence that Ethel had passed on information about the bomb, and some contend she was included in the most serious charge chiefly in an attempt to force her husband to confess. Both Rosenbergs maintained their innocence, however. In 1951 they were tried and eventually condemned to death, a sentence generally reserved for treason during wartime, although they were convicted only of conspiracy to commit espionage in wartime.

It was an extremely high-profile case, both nationally and internationally. By the early 1950s the Cold War was in progress, and there was deep concern about the infiltration of Communists into America. The government and the majority of the public considered this a serious danger and tended to overreact, with the result that many innocent people were accused of being Communist sympathizers. Then, people disturbed by the persecution of the innocent began to think that there were no real Communist spies. The Rosenbergs, however, were admitted Communists who had been active in Communist organizations. The government wanted to make an example of them. Whether their trial was entirely fair is still a matter of debate, although documents that have since been declassified prove that Julius was indeed guilty of passing secrets to the Soviets. The Communists, of course, raised a storm of protest during the years of the trial and the following appeals, and this was joined by many people who were not Communist sympathizers but who believed that to execute the Rosenbergs would be wrong. Emotion ran high on both sides of the issue.

Some claimed that the judge was biased. Some even said he was prejudiced because the Rosenbergs were Jewish, which was ridiculous because he himself was a Jew. Judge Irving Kaufman was deeply convinced that giving away atomic secrets was too serious an offense for light punishment. At the sentencing he said,

> I consider your crime worse than murder.... I believe your conduct in putting into the hands of the Russians the A-bomb years before our best scientists predicted Russia would perfect the bomb has already caused, in my opinion, the Communist aggression in Korea, with the resultant casualties exceeding 50,000 and who knows but that millions more of innocent people may pay the price of your treason. Indeed, by your betrayal you undoubtedly have altered the course of history to the disadvantage of our country. No one can say that we do not live in a constant state of tension. We have evidence of your treachery all around us every day for the civilian defense activities throughout the nation are aimed at preparing us for an atom bomb attack.

After many appeals, and the rejection of pleas for clemency by both presidents Harry Truman and Dwight Eisenhower, the execution was scheduled for June 18, 1953. The day before, an attorney claiming to represent a friend of the Rosenbergs (who was not their official attorney) made one last appeal to the Supreme Court for a stay of execution. He brought up a new issue: he said that because the Atomic Energy Act passed in 1946 did not allow execution unless it was recommended by a jury, the Rosenbergs could not be sentenced under an earlier law that did—even though the crimes of which they were convicted had been committed earlier. Justice William O. Douglas granted the stay, but the next day the Court met in special session and vacated it the following morning. The stay had bought the Rosenbergs one more day, and the executions were carried out on June 19. The Court opinions presented in this chapter were written to explain why the stay was not upheld.

"This stay is not and could not be based upon any doubt that a legal conviction was had under the Espionage Act."

The Court's Decision: No Legal Grounds Exist for Granting the Rosenbergs a Stay of Execution

Robert H. Jackson and Thomas C. Clark

Robert H. Jackson was a justice of the Supreme Court from 1941 to 1951, and Thomas C. Clark was a justice from 1949 to 1967. Both had served as U.S. attorney general prior to appointment to the Court. Their separate opinions that follow were both included in the Court's final disposition of Rosenberg v. United States, *a case not heard by the Court. Justice William O. Douglas had granted a stay of execution two days before, and the Court simply ruled on whether the stay was warranted. The ruling was per curiam (by the court as a whole, rather than an opinion written by one of the justices for the majority). Each justice wrote his own opinion. In his, Jackson argues that the Atomic Energy Act, which became law after some of the Rosenbergs' crimes were committed, does not supersede the Espionage Act under which they were sentenced. Furthermore, he explains, the attorney who requested a stay of execution did not have valid standing to do so. Clark states in his opinion that since the Atomic Energy Act does not cover the specific acts for which the defendants were sentenced, there was no way its lesser penalty could be applied to the case. The Rosenbergs, he main-*

Robert H. Jackson and Tom C. Clark, per curiam opinion, *Rosenberg et ux. v. United States*, U.S. Supreme Court, June 19, 1953. Reproduced by permission.

tains, have brought many appeals before the Court, all of which have been denied, and to grant another delay would be to obstruct the course of justice.

Statement by Robert H. Jackson

This stay was granted upon such legal grounds that this Court cannot allow it to stand as the basis upon which lower courts must conduct further long-drawn proceedings.

The sole ground stated was that the sentence may be governed by the Atomic Energy Act of August 1, 1946, instead of by the earlier Espionage Act. The crime here involved was commenced June 6, 1944. This was more than two years before the Atomic Energy Act was passed. All overt acts relating to atomic energy on which the Government relies took place as early as January 1945.

The Constitution, art. I, sec. 9, prohibits passage of any ex post facto [retroactive] Act. If Congress had tried in 1946 to make transactions of 1944 and 1945 offenses, we would have been obliged to set such an Act aside. To open the door to retroactive criminal statutes would rightly be regarded as a most serious blow to one of the civil liberties protected by our Constitution. Yet the sole ground of this stay is that the Atomic Energy Act may have retrospective application to conspiracies in which the only overt acts were committed before that statute was enacted.

We join in the opinion by Mr. Justice [Thomas C.] Clark and agree that the Atomic Energy Act does not, by text or intention, supersede the earlier Espionage Act. It does not purport to repeal the earlier Act, nor afford any grounds for spelling out a repeal by implication. Each Act is complete in itself and each has its own reason for existence and field of operation. Certainly prosecution, conviction and sentence under the law in existence at the time of the overt acts are not improper. It is obvious that an attempt to prosecute under the later Act would in all probability fail.

This stay is not and could not be based upon any doubt that a legal conviction was had under the Espionage Act. Application here for review of the Court of Appeals decision affirming the conviction was refused and rehearing later denied.

Later, responsible and authorized counsel raised, among other issues, questions as to the sentence, and an application was made for stay until they could be heard. The application was referred to the full Court, with the recommendation that the full Court hold immediate hearing and as an institution make a prompt and final disposition of all questions. This was supported by four Justices and failed for want of one more, Mr. Justice [William] Douglas recording his view that 'there would be no end served by hearing oral argument on the motion for a stay.'

Thus, after being in some form before this Court for over nine months, the merits of all questions raised by the Rosenbergs' counsel had been passed upon, or foreclosed by denials. However, on this application we have heard and decided (since it had been the ground for granting the stay) a new contention, despite the irregular manner in which it was originally presented.

No Valid Standing

This is an important procedural matter of which we disapprove. The stay was granted solely on the petition of one [Irwin] Edelman, who sought to appear as "next friend" of the Rosenbergs. Of course, there is power to allow an appearance in that capacity, under circumstances such as incapacity or isolation from counsel, which make it appropriate to enable the Court to hear a prisoner's case. But in these circumstances the order which grants Edelman's standing further to litigate this case in the lower courts cannot be justified.

Edelman is a stranger to the Rosenbergs and to their case. His intervention was unauthorized by them and originally opposed by their counsel. What may be Edelman's purpose in getting himself into this litigation is not explained, although inquiry was made at the bar. It does not appear that his own record is entirely clear or that he would be a helpful or chosen champion.

The attorneys who appear for Edelman tell us that for two months they tried to get the authorized counsel for the Rosenbergs to raise this issue but were refused. They also inform us that they have eleven more points to present hereafter, although the authorized counsel do not appear to have approved such issues.

The Rosenbergs throughout have had able and zealous counsel of their own choice. These attorneys originally thought this point had no merit and perhaps also that it would obscure the better points on which they were endeavoring to procure a hearing here. Of course, after a Justice of this Court had granted Edelman standing to raise the question and indicated that he is impressed by its substantiality, counsel adopted the argument and it became necessary for us to review it. They also shared their time and the counsel table with the Edelman lawyers thus admitted as attorneys-at-large to their case. The lawyers who have ably and courageously fought the Rosenbergs' battle throughout then listened at this bar to the newly imported counsel make an argument which plainly implied lack of understanding or zeal on the part of the retained counsel. They simply had been elbowed out of the control of their case.

Every lawyer familiar with the workings of our criminal courts and the habits of our bar will agree that this precedent presents a threat to orderly and responsible representation of accused persons and the right of themselves and their counsel to control their own cases. The lower court refused to accept Edelman's intrusion but by the order in question must accept him as having standing to take part in, or to take over, the Rosenbergs' case. That such disorderly intervention is more likely to prejudice than to help the representation of accused persons in highly publicized cases is self-evident. We discountenance this practice.

Vacating this stay is not to be construed as indorsing the wisdom or appropriateness to this case of a death sentence. That sentence, however, is permitted by law and, as was previously pointed out, is therefore not within this Court's power of revision.

Statement by Thomas C. Clark

Seven times now have the defendants been before this Court. In addition, The Chief Justice, as well as individual Justices, have considered applications by the defendants. The Court of Appeals and the District Court have likewise given careful consideration to even more numerous applications than has this Court.

The defendants were sentenced to death on April 5, 1951. Beginning with our refusal to review the conviction and sentence in October 1952, each of the Justices have given the most painstaking consideration to the case. In fact, all during the past Term of this Court one or another facet of this litigation occupied the attention of the Court. At a Special Term on June 15, 1953, we denied for the sixth time the defendants' plea. The next day an application was presented to Mr. Justice Douglas contending that the penalty provisions of the Atomic Energy Act governed this prosecution; and that since the jury did not find that the defendants committed the charged acts with intent to injure the United States nor recommend the imposition of the death penalty the court had no power to impose the sentence of death. After a hearing Mr. Justice Douglas, finding that the contention had merit, granted a stay of execution. The Court convened in Special Term to review that determination.

Human lives are at stake; we need not turn this decision on fine points of procedure or a party's technical standing to claim relief. Nor did Mr. Justice Douglas lack the power and, in view of his firm belief that the legal issues tendered him were substantial, he even had the duty to grant a temporary stay. But for me the short answer to the contention that the Atomic Energy Act of 1946 may invalidate defendants' death sentence is that the Atomic Energy Act cannot here apply. It is true that Section 10(b)(2) and (3) of that Act authorizes capital punishment only upon recommendation of a jury and a finding that the offense was committed with intent to injure the United States. (Notably, by that statute the death penalty may be imposed for peacetime offenses as well, thus exceeding in harshness the penalties provided by the Espionage Act.) This prosecution, however, charged a wartime violation of the Espionage Act of 1917 under which these elements are not prerequisite to a sentence of death. Where Congress by more than one statute proscribes a private course of conduct, the Government may choose to invoke either applicable law: "At least where different proof is required for each offense, a single act or transaction may violate more than one criminal statute." *United States v. Beacon Brass Co.* Nor does the partial overlap of two statutes necessarily work a pro tanto [explicit] repealer of the earlier Act. . . . It is not sufficient "to establish that subsequent laws cover some or even all of the cases provided for by (the prior act); for they may be merely affirmative, or cumulative, or auxiliary". There must be "a positive repugnancy between the provisions of the new law and those of the old". *United States v. Borden Co.* Otherwise the Government when charging a conspiracy to transmit both atomic and non-atomic secrets would have to split its prosecution into two alleged crimes. Section 10(b)(6) of the Atomic Energy Act itself, moreover, expressly provides that section 10 "shall not exclude the applicable provisions of any other laws," an unmistakable reference to the 1917 Espionage Act. Therefore this section of the Atomic Energy Act, instead of repealing the penalty provisions of the Espionage Act, in fact preserves them in undiminished force. Thus there is no warrant for superimposing the penalty provisions of the later Act upon the earlier law.

Newer Law Not Retroactive

In any event, the Government could not have invoked the Atomic Energy Act against these defendants. The crux of the charge alleged overt acts committed in 1944 and 1945, years before that Act went into effect. While some overt acts did in fact take place as late as 1950, they related principally to defendants' efforts to avoid detection and prosecution of earlier deeds. Grave doubts of unconstitutional ex post facto criminality would have attended any prosecution under that statute for transmitting atomic secrets before 1946. Since the Atomic Energy Act thus cannot cover the offenses charged, the alleged inconsistency of its penalty provisions with those of the Espionage Act cannot be sustained.

Our liberty is maintained only so long as justice is secure. To permit our judicial processes to be used to obstruct the course of justice destroys our freedom. Over two years ago the Rosenbergs were found guilty by a jury of a grave offense in time of war. Unlike other litigants they have had the attention of this Court seven times; each time their pleas have been denied. Though the penalty is great and our responsibility heavy, our duty is clear.

> "No man or woman should go to death under an unlawful sentence merely because his lawyer failed to raise the point."

Dissenting Opinion: Execution of the Rosenbergs Would Be Unlawful

William O. Douglas

William O. Douglas, who was a member of the Supreme Court from 1936 to 1975, was the longest-serving justice in the Court's history. He was a strong civil libertarian and supporter of First Amendment rights. It was he who issued the temporary stay of execution of Julius and Ethel Rosenberg, which was overturned by the Court as a whole. He wrote the following dissent as part of the Court's final opinion issued after the execution. In it, he maintains that after the Court's discussion he is even more sure that he was right in his interpretation of the law. It is irrelevant that the Rosenbergs' crime took place mainly before the passage of a new law not allowing execution without a jury recommendation, he says. When there are two laws that can apply to a case, a court has no choice but to impose the less harsh of the two sentences allowed.

When the motion for a stay was before me, I was deeply troubled by the legal question tendered. After twelve hours of research and study I concluded, as my opinion indicated, that the question was a substantial one, never presented to this Court and never decided by any court. So I issued the stay order.

William O. Douglas, dissenting opinion, *Rosenberg et ux. v. United States*, U.S. Supreme Court, June 19, 1953. Reproduced by permission.

Now I have had the benefit of an additional argument and additional study and reflection. Now I know that I am right on the law.

The Solicitor General says in oral argument that the Government would have been laughed out of court if the indictment in this case had been laid under the Atomic Energy Act of 1946. I agree. For a part of the crime alleged and proved antedated that Act. And obviously no criminal statute can have retroactive application. But the Solicitor General misses the legal point on which my stay order was based. It is this— whether or not the death penalty can be imposed without the recommendation of the jury for a crime involving the disclosure of atomic secrets where a part of that crime takes place after the effective date of the Atomic Energy Act.

The crime of the Rosenbergs was a conspiracy that started prior to the Atomic Energy Act and continued almost 4 years after the effective date of that Act. The overt acts alleged were acts which took place prior to the effective date of the new Act. But that is irrelevant for two reasons. First, acts in pursuance of the conspiracy were proved which took place after the new Act became the law. Second, under *Singer v. United States*, no overt acts were necessary; the crime was complete when the conspiracy was proved. And that conspiracy, as defined in the indictment itself, endured almost 4 years after the Atomic Energy Act became effective.

The crime therefore took place in substantial part after the new Act became effective, after Congress had written new penalties for conspiracies to disclose atomic secrets. One of the new requirements is that the death penalty for that kind of espionage can be imposed only if the jury recommends it. And here there was no such recommendation. To be sure, this espionage included more than atomic secrets. But there can be no doubt that the death penalty was imposed because of the Rosenbergs' disclosure of atomic secrets. The trial judge, in sentencing the Rosenbergs to death, emphasized that the heinous character of their crime was trafficking in atomic secrets. He said:

> I believe your conduct in putting into the hands of the Russians the A bomb years before our best scientists predicted Russia would perfect the bomb has already caused, in my opinion, the Communist aggression in Korea, with the resultant casualties exceeding 50,000 and who knows but that millions more of innocent people may pay the price of your treason. Indeed, by your betrayal you undoubtedly have altered the course of history to the disadvantage of our country.

The New Law

But the Congress in 1946 adopted new criminal sanctions for such crimes. Whether Congress was wise or unwise in doing so is no question for us. The cold truth is that the death sentence may not be imposed for what the Rosenbergs did unless the jury so recommends.

Some say, however, that since a part of the Rosenbergs' crime was committed under the old law, the penalties of the old law apply. But it is law too elemental for citation of authority that where two penal statutes may apply—one carrying death, the other imprisonment—the court has no choice but to impose the less harsh sentence.

A suggestion is made that the question comes too late, that since the Rosenbergs did not raise this question on appeal, they are barred from raising it now. But the question of an unlawful sentence is never barred. No man or woman should go to death under an unlawful sentence merely because his lawyer failed to raise the point. It is that function among others that the Great Writ [habeas corpus] serves. I adhere to the views stated by Chief Justice [Charles Evans] Hughes for a unanimous Court in *Bowen v. Johnston*:

It must never be forgotten that the writ of habeas corpus is the precious safeguard of personal liberty and there is no higher duty than to maintain it unimpaired. . . . The rule requiring resort to appellate procedure when the trial court has determined its own jurisdiction of an offense is not a rule denying the power to issue a writ of habeas corpus when it appears that nevertheless the trial court was without jurisdiction. The rule is not one defining power but one which relates to the appropriate exercise of power.

Here the trial court was without jurisdiction to impose the death penalty, since the jury had not recommended it.

Before the present argument I knew only that the question was serious and substantial. Now I am sure of the answer. I know deep in my heart that I am right on the law. Knowing that, my duty is clear.

"The political and social upheaval surrounding the [Rosenberg] trial . . . can only be understood through the lens of heightened Cold War tensions."

The Rosenberg Case Bred Controversy During the Cold War

Adrienne Wilmoth Lerner

Adrienne Wilmoth Lerner is a lawyer and the executive director of LernerMedia. She has written many articles and edited several books. In the following article she explains the case of Julius and Ethel Rosenberg, who were executed in 1953 for operating a spy ring that gave the plans for the atomic bomb to the Soviet Union. Other spies, including Ethel Rosenberg's brother, had been arrested earlier and had accused them. They maintained their innocence and their case drew a great deal of national attention; it led to major demonstrations protesting the alleged unfairness of their trial and death sentence. Emotions were strong on both sides, and the case continues to stir controversy. Recently declassified documents have shown that the evidence against them was overwhelming, but, Lerner contends, the political and social impact of the case resulted from the anti-Communist hysteria of the day.

Julius and Ethel Rosenberg were a couple accused in 1950 by the United States government of operating a Soviet spy network and giving the Soviet Union plans for the atomic bomb.

Adrienne Wilmoth Lerner, "Rosenberg (Ethel and Julius) Espionage Case," in *Encyclopedia of Espionage, Intelligence and Security*, ed. K. Lee Lerner and Brenda Wilmoth Lerner, vol. 3. Farmington Hills, MI: Gale, 2004, pp. 29–30. Copyright © 2004 by Gale. Reproduced by permission of Gale, a part of Cengage Learning.

During a time of tense scrutiny over alleged communist infiltration of the American government, the trial of the Rosenbergs became the center of a political storm over communist influence in America. Their trial was one of the most controversial of the twentieth century, ending with their execution.

Julius Rosenberg was a committed communist who had graduated from the City College of New York in 1939 with a degree in electrical engineering. He married Ethel Greenglass in the summer of that year. She was a headstrong woman, active in organizing labor groups. Julius had opened a mechanic shop with his brother-in-law, but the business soon began to fail, largely due to lack of attention by Julius, who invested his time spying for the Soviets. He began by stealing manuals for radar tubes and proximity fuses, and by the late 1940s, had two apartments set up as microfilm laboratories.

The arrest of the Rosenbergs was set in motion when the FBI arrested Klaus Fuchs, a British scientist who gave atomic secrets to the Soviets while working on the Manhattan Project [to develop the atom bomb]. Fuchs's arrest and confession led to the arrest of Harry Gold, a courier for Soviet spies. Gold in turn led investigators to David Greenglass, a minor spy who confessed quickly. Greenglass then accused his sister Ethel and brother-in-law Julius of controlling his activities.

Julius immediately realized the implications of Harry Gold's arrest and began to make arrangements to get out of the country, but the FBI moved swiftly. Julius Rosenberg was arrested in July 1950.

Ethel Rosenberg was later arrested in August. Although Federal investigators had little evidence against her, they hoped to use the threat of prosecuting her as a lever to persuade Julius to confess. The plan failed, and the couple was charged with conspiracy to commit espionage. Their trial began on March 6, 1951.

Trial Drew National Attention

From the beginning, the trial attracted national attention. The prosecution decided to keep the scope of the trial as narrow as possible, with establishing the Rosenbergs' guilt the main target, and exposing their spy ring a lesser concern. Nonetheless, the trial was punctuated by numerous arrests of spies associated with the Rosenbergs, some appearing in court to testify against them.

The defense tried to downplay the importance of the information the prosecution claimed the Rosenbergs had stolen, but then turned around and requested that all spectators and reporters be barred from the courtroom when the information was discussed.

The Rosenbergs accused David Greenglass of turning on them because of their failed business, but these efforts only elicited sympathy for a man who had been forced to turn in a family member. Greenglass damaged the Rosenbergs by testifying that Julius had arranged for him to give Harry Gold the design of the atomic bomb used on Nagasaki (which differed considerably from the Hiroshima bomb). When Gold himself testified, he named Anatoli Yakovlev as his contact. This directly tied the Rosenbergs to a known Soviet agent. Julius and Ethel Rosenberg were found guilty on several accounts of espionage and conspiracy. They were sentenced to execution, a sentence usually reserved for cases of treason.

After months in prison, the Rosenbergs still maintained their innocence and began to write poignant letters, which were widely published, protesting their treatment. The case was followed closely in Europe, where many felt the Rosenbergs were being persecuted because they were Jewish (though Judge [Irving] Kaufman was also Jewish). A movement began to protest the "injustice" of the Rosenberg trial. Passions both for and against the Rosenbergs grew so great that they even threatened Franco-American relations, as the French were particularly harsh in their condemnation of the trial as a sham.

Major Demonstrations Held

In the months between the sentencing and execution, criticism of the trial grew more strident, and major demonstrations were held. Nobel-prize winner Jean-Paul Sartre called the case "a legal lynching which smears with blood a whole nation." In spite of attempts at appeal and a temporary stay issued by Supreme Court Justice William O. Douglas, Julius and Ethel Rosenberg were executed on June 19, 1953, both refusing to confess.

Years after the event, the case continues to stir debate. Although the Rosenbergs were communists and engaged in espionage, they did not spy for an enemy of the United States, as the sentence might indicate, but rather for its wartime ally. Recent studies of the couple's activities show that the evidence against them was overwhelming. The declassification and release of Venona transcripts (a secret, decades-long, general surveillance operation) further implicated the Rosenbergs. Regardless of the evidence, the political and social upheaval surrounding the trial, and its ultimate outcome, can only be understood through the lens of heightened Cold War tensions and anti-Communist hysteria.

> *"[The Rosenbergs' trial judge] made ex-*
> *traordinary efforts to expedite the ex-*
> *ecutions and to frustrate the appeal*
> *process by denying* habeas corpus . . .
> *[and] by communicating secretly with*
> *. . . the prosecution."*

The Rosenbergs' Constitutional Rights Were Violated

National Committee to Reopen the Rosenberg Case

The National Committee to Reopen the Rosenberg Case
(NCRRC) was formed approximately ten years after the execu-
tion of Julius and Ethel Rosenberg in 1953 and has been con-
tinuously in existence ever since. In the following viewpoint the
NCRRC presents its view of the circumstances under which the
Rosenbergs were executed. After a detailed discussion of the al-
leged unfairness of the trial (which due to space limitations is
not included here), the NCRRC declares that the judge was bi-
ased because he was a known hater of Communists and that he
had promised the government in advance to impose the death
sentence. The committee also states that in order to close the case
quickly, the justices of the Supreme Court improperly made
agreements among themselves and with the attorney general not
to consider granting a stay of execution.

What was the emotional and political climate in America
when the Rosenberg trial took place? Fear, paranoia,
and anti-communist hysteria were rampant throughout the
country. How had this come to happen?

"Setting the Stage: Case for the Defense," rosenbergtrial.org. Reproduced by permission.

America had ended World War II by dropping atomic bombs on the Japanese cities of Hiroshima and Nagasaki. After a decade of depression and four years of wartime shortages, Americans looked forward to an age of prosperity and military security; an age of peace and tranquility and the blessings of democracy. We were the only nation not to have suffered massive damages from the war and we had THE BOMB. *Pax Americana* [peace resulting from the superior power of America] was just around the corner.

However, only four years later, in the Fall of 1949, things were drastically different. Our ex-ally the Soviet Union, which had occupied and was now ruling much of eastern Europe, had erected an *iron curtain* [a term referring both to physical barriers and an ideological one] that divided East from West. On the home front, efforts were accelerating to protect the United States from the influence of the Soviets' communist ideology. From the loyalty oath program put in place for federal employees, to the investigations by the House Un-American Activities Committee and others like it, anyone considered to be a communist or to have communist affiliations, was vilified and considered to be a threat to the United States. More specifically, in contradiction to what our top nuclear scientists claimed, government officials declared that our "atomic secrets" must be protected. Americans should be on the lookout for any suspicious behavior by communists who might give away the secret of the atom bomb.

In September of 1949, whatever sense of security was left had been shattered when President [Harry S.] Truman announced that the Soviets had exploded their own atomic bomb. Suddenly the stakes were much higher and the communist threat much greater. Now we had to solve the riddle of how the USSR had been able to develop their own A-bomb. The only answer that seemed reasonable was that it had to be due to atomic espionage. A massive search was initiated to find the spies responsible for this heinous act of treachery.

In June of 1950, the Korean war began and American soldiers were being killed by the communist aggressors in Asia. It was widely thought at that time that the war had started because the Soviet-backed communists of North Korea were emboldened when the USSR had exploded its own A-bomb.

The threat of communism was perceived to be so great that the McCarran Internal Security Act was passed by an 83 percent majority of Congress over the strenuous veto of President Truman. Among other things, the Act declared that to be a communist meant that one's allegiance was to the Soviet Union and not to the United States. It also provided that in an emergency situation, citizens could be imprisoned merely on the suspicion that they *might* engage in criminal activities.

The prevailing tensions of being at war combined with the rising anxiety regarding communism was reflected by the *media frenzy* that preceded the Rosenberg trial. Daily, the details of the gory carnage our troops were suffering in Asia was reported alongside the unfolding story of the "atom spies" who had been captured and were to be tried for what J. Edger Hoover described as "the crime of the century." It was in this milieu of fear and anger that the Rosenbergs entered the courtroom. . . .

The Trial Judge Was Biased

Judge [Irving] Kaufman contaminated the judicial process. This occurred before, during and after the trial. Any semblance of judicial impartiality ended *before* the start of the trial. Judge Kaufman, a known hater of Communists, actively campaigned to be assigned to this case. An FBI document indicates that part of the reason that he was chosen to adjudicate this case was that he assured officials in the Justice Department that he would impose the death sentence if warranted. Indeed this same document shows that this kind of unlawful *ex parte* [outside the trial proceedings] communication, where a judge discusses the case with the prosecution but without the presence of the defense, continued throughout the trial.

His strong bias is next demonstrated during the jury selection process. During the trial, Judge Kaufman behaved as if he was an additional member of the prosecution team. . . .

Thus, in one of their appeal briefs, the defense stated that the Judge had taken too active and biased a role in the proceedings, depriving the defendants of a fair trial. Legally however, a federal judge can take a much more active role in a trial than a state judge can. Although the appellate court opinion actually cited many incidents . . . it still ruled that Judge Kaufman stayed within the discretion allowed him.

FBI documents show that Kaufman made extraordinary efforts to expedite the executions and to frustrate the appeal process by denying *habeas corpus* relief [determination of unlawful imprisonment] without hearing, by communicating secretly with members of the prosecution staff, the FBI, and through them, with the Department of Justice.

For example: the record reveals that the last application of the Rosenbergs to set aside their sentences was made in June, 1953. It came to be heard before Judge Kaufman and was summarily denied *without affording any evidentiary hearing.* The record also reveals that prior to the time the motion was even filed, subject matter of the motion was secretly discussed at a meeting between Hoover and Judge Kaufman in May of 1953. The prosecution thereafter briefed him as to the issues that might be raised before the motion was made, thus permitting the summary denial. . . .

Prejudiced Jury Selection

The McCarran Internal Security Act of 1950 was passed just months *after* the Rosenbergs were arrested. This act was passed by Congress (84%) over President Truman's veto. (Truman considered the Act unconstitutional which was later confirmed in the courts by 1971.) The Act held that all members of the Communist Party, and all members of 100 organizations listed by the Attorney General as *Communist Front* organizations (over half of a million Americans), are in effect agents of the Soviet Union.

Kaufman was one of the first judges to utilize the McCarran Act in the courtroom. In eliminating potential jurors, Kaufman not only used the criteria of membership in the list of organizations specified by the McCarran Act, but *added* several "communist front" organizations of his own choosing. He then further extended dismissal to include *former members* and *friends and family* of any members of these organizations. Thus, thousands of potential jurors with liberal or progressive viewpoints were eliminated from consideration. . . .

Supreme Court Was Compromised

It is Monday, June 15, 1953; just three days before the scheduled electrocutions of the Rosenbergs. It is also the last day the Supreme Court would meet before adjourning for its summer vacation. In a highly improper "gentleman's agreement," the nine justices agreed that *any new motions, regardless of merit*, pertaining to the Rosenberg case, would not be considered. This agreement was no doubt due to the tremendous pressure exerted upon the court by external events and the bitter internal haggling about the Rosenberg case that had persisted for so long. However, this collusion was not just an unorthodox oddity at the end of a trying term. Joseph Sharlitt, author of *Fatal Error* comments: ". . . private agreements among judges that dispose of serious points of law before they are made do violence to our system of justice." In the coming days, things would get much worse.

In meetings documented by the FBI, Justices [Fred] Vinson and [Robert] Jackson privately met with Attorney General [Herbert] Brownell to discuss what actions would be taken if Justices [William] Douglas or [Felix] Frankfurter were to break the gentleman's agreement. They knew that Douglas or Frankfurter was considering a petition by [attorneys] Fyke Farmer and Daniel Marshall pertaining to the Rosenberg case. On Tuesday, June 16, Vinson, Jackson, and Brownell agreed that if Douglas submitted a stay of execution in order to have the Farmer-Marshall petition considered, they would immediately convene a special session of the court to overturn the stay. Furthermore, at Brownell's suggestion, Chief Justice Vinson agreed to meet privately with Douglas and try to convince him not to decide the merits of the new motion himself, but to submit the motion for consideration in conference (Brownell knew that in conference, the petition would be dismissed by a majority of the judges).

Meetings of this type (between Brownell and Vinson) are called *ex parte communication*, and are strictly forbidden by the canons of ethics for both judges and lawyers. Any meeting between judge and prosecutor, pertaining to a case at hand, which does not also include a member of the defense, is unethical and improper.

The repercussions of these meetings were to result in perhaps a low point of judicial conduct by the court. Vinson actually met with Douglas and tried to persuade him to not consider the merits of the Farmer-Marshall petition himself. After this failed, and Douglas issued a stay on June 17th, the *ex parte* Brownell-Jackson-Vinson contingency plan was put into motion.

On June 18th, for only the third time in its history, the Supreme Court was reconvened after adjournment for vacation. (Neither the defense attorneys nor Justice Douglas were notified that this meeting was to take place.) And for the *first time in its history*, a stay by one of the judges was vacated by the other members of the court. Supreme Court scholars are still unclear as to whether such an action is even legal.

But for the Rosenbergs, such debates are moot. Their executions were carried out on Friday, June 19th, just one day after this unprecedented action by the Supreme Court. The corruption in the Rosenberg case had reached the highest court in our land. ·

> "Probably no jurist has ever probed
> deeper into his own conscience than
> Irving Robert Kaufman, ... who pre-
> sided over the world-famous trial of
> Ethel and Julius Rosenberg."

The Judge Acted Conscientiously in Sentencing the Rosenbergs to Death

Milton Lehman

Milton Lehman was a writer who contributed hundreds of articles to national magazines. He also wrote a biography of rocket pioneer Robert H. Goddard. In the following article, written shortly after the execution of Julius and Ethel Rosenberg, he tells about the ordeal of federal judge Irving Kaufman, the man who sentenced them to death. Kaufman's conscience was deeply troubled by the case, Lehman claims, yet he believed that they were tried fairly and that both justice and the best interests of the nation demanded the death sentence. Though many people praised Judge Kaufman for his courage, he also heard from many who felt that to kill the Rosenbergs would be wrong; moreover, he was the target of a vicious campaign launched by Communist organizations and their sympathizers and even received threats to his family. Through it all, Lehman contends, Kaufman remained convinced that he had made the right decision.

Milton Lehman, "The Rosenberg Case: Judge Kaufman's Two Terrible Years," *Saturday Evening Post*, August 8, 1953. Copyright © 1953 Saturday Evening Post Society. Reproduced by permission.

For every judge there eventually comes a case which the law alone cannot resolve, which sends him to the depths of his soul for decision. Probably no jurist has ever probed deeper into his own conscience than Irving Robert Kaufman, United States judge of the Southern District Court of New York, who presided over the world-famous trial of Ethel and Julius Rosenberg, atomic spies. In the Rosenberg case, which came to him in March, 1951, it ultimately fell to Judge Kaufman to sentence the defendants to death. Thus for Kaufman began long months of anguish. . . . For the Rosenbergs the sad drama ended on the evening of June 19, 1953, when they died in the electric chair at the Sing Sing death house. But the Rosenberg sentence, perhaps the most significant in our time, will be argued for years to come.

In its last moments the Rosenberg case reached a cloud-land of legal arguments and world-wide emotion which blanketed the essentials of the trial more than two years before. First, the Rosenbergs were found guilty by jury of conspiracy to commit espionage for the Soviet Union in time of war. Second, the Rosenbergs refused is admit their guilt despite overwhelming evidence that they had delivered to Russia certain vital secrets of the atomic bomb. Third, they were charged with violating the Federal Espionage Act of 1917, a statute which gave the trial judge an unusually binding choice of sentences: imprisonment up to thirty years and beyond that only death. Fourth, the trial judge found no alternative to the death decree, making the Rosenbergs the first American spies ever sentenced to death in peacetime by a United States civil court.

After Judge Kaufman's sentence, the Rosenberg case was merely begun. It became the most-appealed Federal trial in recent history. The Rosenbergs' pleas were repeatedly heard, considered and rejected: sixteen times by the Southern District Court of New York, seven times by the Second Circuit Court of Appeals, seven times by the Supreme Court of the United States, which made its final ruling on the day of execution. Beyond the Supreme Court, the Rosenbergs' appeals for executive clemency were passed up by President [Harry] Truman and twice flatly rejected by his successor, President [Dwight] Eisenhower.

The Rosenbergs' service to Soviet Russia began with espionage. Silence and death were their final service. They never gave the United States the assistance in detecting other betrayers that might have brought them mercy. Instead, they gave their names to a major communist campaign in the cold war against free society, a campaign to mislead the minds, trick the emotions and probe the soft spots of irresponsibility in free men around the world.

Before the communist bombast, the free world showed signs of panic. In France, President Vincent Auriol and three former premiers relayed their appeals for clemency to President Eisenhower. While the British Government held firm, thousands of British subjects cabled the American courts demanding mercy for the Rosenbergs. Eight Dutch jurists asked for clemency. Eighteen rabbis in Israel appealed for the Rosenbergs' lives, although several of them later withdrew their names. Pope Pius XII, without stating his own sentiments, advised the White House of the extraordinary appeals to him to save the Rosenbergs.

Witch-Hunt and Frame-Up Charges

In the United States, many Americans who accepted the Rosenbergs' guilt protested their execution: ministers and other citizens who opposed the death sentence for any crime, physicists such as Dr. Albert Einstein and Dr. Harold C. Urey, who helped to create the atomic bomb and were deeply disturbed by their creature: fearful diplomats who believed the impending Rosenberg "martyrdom" was a permanent cold-war weapon; and warm-hearted people who felt the plight of the Rosenberg children more keenly than their own plight under a possible Russian atomic attack.

The Rosenberg case troubled millions of free men, but none so much as Judge Irving Kaufman, the only man who was fully responsible for their death sentence. While many Americans praised him and some proposed that he run for governor of New York State, others called him a murderer and proposed that he run for his life. At first, the communists' twisted charges—"witch-hunt," "frame-up," "anti-Semitism"— bothered him little; he knew they were nonsense. But later they captured the minds of loyal men, stirred their emotions and came back to haunt him. Bound to judicial silence, Kaufman at first felt a gnawing desire to answer his critics. After a time, he discovered that his own critical faculties were turning most sharply against himself.

Obviously there was no witch-hunt in the Rosenberg case. They were fairly tried and given unusual opportunities for appeal. But might a judge, Kaufman wondered, somehow be swayed by the current anxiety over communism beyond the actual dangers of the crime? Had he ruled solely on the trial evidence and sentenced with his mind clearly on the law and the meaning of the crime? It was absurd to accuse him of anti-Semitism. After all, Kaufman himself was a devout Jew. But might a Jew somehow fail to be just, might he lean over backward in severity toward other Jews? In the months that followed, Kaufman faced and resolved such questions in silence. . . .

The Trial

In the Southern District a trial judge takes his turn in rotation, presiding over criminal, civil, admiralty, motions and naturalization proceedings. In March, 1951, Kaufman was sitting in criminal court when Chief Judge John Knox sent him for trial in the case of the United States of America vs. Julius Rosenberg, Ethel Rosenberg, Anatoli A. Yakovlev, David Greenglass and Morton Sobell. The defendants were charged with espionage in wartime. . . .

If Judge Kaufman wished to stay inconspicuous as a fresh-man on the bench, this was scarcely a trial to hide behind. The press covered it in fullest detail and Kaufman's name made most editions of most newspapers across the country. Only one New York newspaper, in fact, considered the trial unworthy of notice—the *Daily Worker* of the United States Communist Party.

As the conspiracy unfolded, the Government's case against the Rosenbergs seemed overwhelming. . . .

The defense offered nothing but denials of guilt. On the stand, Julius and then Ethel Rosenberg were glib and self-assured as they supplied a flat refrain to their attorney's questions . . . : "I did not. . . . I did not," To all the Government's questions about alleged communist activities, they called on the Fifth Amendment to the Constitution: "I refuse to answer on the grounds that it may tend to incriminate me." The third defendant, Morton Sobell, declined to testify and rested his case on the record.

On March twenty-ninth, the three week trial was over. After seven hours and forty-two minutes of deliberation the jury returned a verdict of guilty against the Rosenbergs and Sobell Judge Kaufman reserved sentence for one week, ordering the court adjourned until the morning of April fifth.

Most of that week, Kaufman stayed in his chambers, reading the court's transcript and probing the issues of the case. As he revealed in a later opinion, there were three chief considerations. First was the law itself. The Espionage Act provided for wartime espionage a sentence of imprisonment up to thirty years and beyond that only death. It was an old statute, drawn up by Congress in 1917, when the United States had no secret remotely as important as the atomic bomb. The lawmakers seemed to say that wartime espionage was serious enough for limited imprisonment or else so serious as to call for death. The judge must make that determination.

Second was the magnitude of the crime. The Rosenbergs were found specifically guilty of atomic spying. The Congressional Joint Committee on Atomic Energy estimated that the atomic spies, including Greenglass, had advanced Russia's ability to produce an atomic bomb by at least eighteen months.

Third was the interest of the two parties to the trial. A judge must be merciful to the individual, given any reason for mercy. He is also bound to protect the large, sometimes vague and always vital rights of society. What sentence would be just and also provide the maximum deterrent effect against such crimes in the future? A thirty-year sentence made the offender legally eligible for parole after ten years. A death sentence, once carried out, was irrevocable. . . .

On the day before sentence, Kaufman agreed to see Mrs. Tessie Greenglass, the mother of David and Ethel, who had been pleading for an interview. An older judge, hearing of his intention, stopped him in the courthouse elevator and put an arm around Kaufman's shoulder. "Don't do it, Irving," he said. "You're just putting yourself through a wringer."

Kaufman answered wearily, "She's entitled to see me." . . .

Next morning in the large, hushed courtroom, Judge Kaufman sentenced Julius and Ethel Rosenberg to death. "Your crime is worse than murder," he said. "Plain, deliberate, contemplated murder is dwarfed in magnitude by comparison with the crime you have committed. . . . I feel that I must pass . . . [a] sentence which will demonstrate with finality that this nation's security must remain inviolate." He sentenced Morton Sobell to thirty years in prison, because there was no evidence of atomic espionage in his case. . . .

The Campaign Against Kaufman

After the sentencing, Kaufman was exhausted. With Thomas Dodd, of Hartford, Connecticut, an old colleague who later became a congressman, he flew down to Palm Beach, Florida. . . .

Back in New York, Kaufman found hundreds of telegrams and letters praising his decision. Wherever he went he was recognized. . . .

Kaufman discovered that no matter what his court assignment might be, he was still "the judge in the Rosenberg case." With every defense appeal, his name appeared in the newspapers. His most casual acquaintances brought up the case. As a result, Kaufman withdrew from all but his family and closest friends. . . .

In time, even his friends agreed that Kaufman had a monumental cause for concern; he had become a world-wide target for one of the noisiest campaigns ever waged against an American judge.

The campaign to "save the Rosenbergs" was conducted on two levels. The legal maneuvers were handled by Emanuel Bloch, the Rosenbergs' aggressive defense attorney. In October, 1951, Bloch applied to the Second Circuit Court of Appeals for judicial review. Asking for a new trial, he charged that Judge Kaufman had been prejudiced and that his conduct of the trial deprived the Rosenbergs of a fair hearing. The Circuit Court, after weeks of study, rejected Bloch's appeal. He took it on to the Supreme Court, which also turned it down. Until the case ended in the Sing Sing death house, Bloch returned again and again to the courts with legal arguments that were dismissed as baseless, charging perjury by witnesses, judicial prejudice, improper trial conduct and a harsh and unwarranted sentence.

Following these arguments, Judge Kaufman recalled the tributes Bloch had paid him in open court at the end of the trial, "We feel you have treated us with the utmost courtesy," Bloch said then. . . . "We feel the trial has been conducted . . . with that dignity and decorum that befits an American trial. . . . The court has conducted itself as an American judge."

Bloch succeeded three times in staying the date of execution set by Judge Kaufman. And while Bloch gained time, the communists developed the Rosenberg case into a major propaganda weapon. Obviously, they knew that the Rosenbergs were "dependable," that they would never talk even to save their lives. With this assurance, the National Committee to Secure Justice in the Rosenberg Case opened its campaign in 1952. Describing itself as "spontaneously organized," the committee was immediately supported by communist fronts. . . .

Leading off with the charge of "anti-Semitism," the Rosenberg committee counted on driving a wedge of doubt between the democracy and one of its minorities. Responsible Jewish organizations such as the American Jewish Committee and the Anti-Defamation League of B'nai Brith vigorously condemned the committee. Anti-Semitism was absolutely no issue in the Rosenberg case, they said, but rather a coldly deliberate attempt to confuse public opinion and take the heat off Russia's genuine anti-Semitic purges. The committee's second major charge was "frame-up" and "witch-hunt." This charge was repeated often enough for the American Civil Liberties Union to conduct an independent investigation. They reported no violation of civil liberties. . . .

Toward the end of 1952, the efforts of Bloch and the Rosenberg committee brought a flood of angry letters and telegrams to Judge Kaufman, some of them saying: "If the Rosenbergs die, none but you will be the murderer." . . . "In this life and any hereafter, may you be damned." . . . "May your children become orphans."

Divided Public Opinion

Kaufman knew that many sincere people opposed his sentence as too severe and were deeply distressed. Late in October, 1952, he received a letter from Rabbi Emanuel Rackman, of Far Rockaway, Long Island. The rabbi, a one-time law student, had closely investigated the Rosenberg case and read the full trial record. A few days after sending his letter, the rabbi was surprised to received a call inviting him to come to Kaufman's chambers. . . .

Later, Rabbi Rackman recalled his meeting with Kaufman, "I had the feeling that Judge Kaufman had really suffered," he said. "There was nothing harsh or vindictive in the man. He believed deeply that the United States must draw an indelible line against such crimes for its own safety. Thousands of people had urged him to be merciful, but he felt that such appeals should be addressed to the Rosenbergs, who still had the power to repent. They had violently betrayed their country, he felt, and their refusal to aid their Government as others had, offered him no grounds for mercy. But I still felt troubled by the death sentence and I said so to the judge."

The Rackman interview was one more indication to Kaufman that many loyal Americans did not see the Rosenberg case as he did. He had received full support from most of the public; the vast majority of attorneys and judges approved his decision, and said so; the higher courts had repeatedly upheld him; Tau Epsilon Phi, his college fraternity, had named him "Man of the Year"; and B'nai Brith had cited him for "furthering the cause of democratic freedom." Nevertheless, Kaufman felt nagged by the public's uneasiness and wished he could show all Americans, step by step, why he considered the Rosenberg sentence not only just but inevitable.

In December, 1952, Bloch once more came before Judge Kaufman, appealing for judicial clemency and reduction in the Rosenberg sentence. . . .

[Kaufman] delivered his opinion on January 2, 1958, almost two years after the original Rosenberg trial. In it, he reviewed the case in detail, explained the Federal statute and its meaning, considered the crime and sentence from both the narrow legal sense and the broader implications.

"I still feel that their crime was worse than murder," he observed. "Their traitorous acts were of the highest degree. They turned over information to Russia concerning the most deadly weapon known to man, thereby exposing millions of their countrymen to danger or death. The Rosenbergs were not minor espionage agents; they were on the top rung of this conspiracy." . . .

Their lips have remained sealed and they prefer the glory which they believe will be theirs by the martyrdom which will be bestowed upon them by those who enlisted them in this diabolical conspiracy (and who, indeed, desire them to remain silent). . . . The defendants, still defiant, assert that they seek justice, not mercy. What they seek, they have attained.

"Despite this," Kaufman went on, "I must nevertheless consider whether they are deserving of mercy. While I am deeply moved by considerations of parenthood and while I find death in form heartrending, I have a responsibility to mete out justice in a manner dictated by the statutes and the interests of our country. My personal feelings or preferences must be pushed aside, for my prime obligation is to society and to American institutions."

Finally, Judge Kaufman declared, "I have meditated and re-flected long and difficult hours over the sentence in this case. I have studied and restudied the record and I have seen noth-ing, nor has anything been presented to me to cause me to change the sentence originally imposed. . . . Nor have I seen any evidence that the defendants have experienced any re-morse or repentance. . . .

"The application is denied."

Demonstrations and Threats

In the last days before the execution, the Rosenberg case reached a peak of emotional suspense. Around the world, Rosenberg supporters staged demonstrations outside United States embassies and consulates. Three days before the execu-tion, communist Poland offered asylum to the Rosenbergs if the United States would let them go. The State Department said Poland's proposal was "beneath reply." And in Washing-ton, 6800 pickets marched outside the White House, bearing placards urging the President to commute the death sentence. In their midst were the Rosenberg sons, Michael and Robert.

Meanwhile, the American judicial system had reached its noblest hour. There was great confusion over the intense, complex legal arguments that brought an unprecedented last-minute stay of execution from Supreme Court Justice William O. Douglas. The Douglas decision of Wednesday, June seventeenth, resulted from the appeal of a curious little man named Irwin Edelman, who had no connection with the case, but presented himself as "next friend" to the Rosenbergs. Edelman was a middle-aged soap-box orator who had been thrown out of the Communist Party for criticizing its leadership. He had been jailed a dozen times for begging, disturbing the peace, vagrancy and malicious mischief. Edelman, through two attorneys, argued that the Rosenbergs had been convicted under the wrong statute. His argument appealed to Justice Douglas as meriting further review. In the Rosenberg case, Edelman seemed the least likely man to concern the nation's highest court. But to the smallest sparrow, the American judiciary system responded as if to the mightiest eagle.

The Supreme Court, adjourned for the summer, was recalled in extraordinary session on Thursday, June eighteenth, to consider the action of Justice Douglas. They withheld decision that night, the time set for the Rosenberg execution, thereby giving the Rosenbergs another day of life. At noon on Friday, June nineteenth, they overruled Justice Douglas by a vote of 6 to 2, declaring that the Edelman appeal lacked substance.

In his chambers on Foley Square, Judge Irving Kaufman sat and waited for the last developments. In his outer office were two FBI agents, sitting quietly with their hats beside them, like counselors calling on business. The agents had been sitting in much the same position all that week. Other FBI men were assigned to Kaufman's family, to guard his wife and children. During the week, the police got two false reports of time bombs planted in the Kaufman apartment house. Each time they sent their bomb squads to investigate.

The Final Outcome

In midafternoon Judge Kaufman heard from the United States marshal at Sing Sing that the Rosenberg execution would occur before sundown, in respect for the beginning of the Jewish sabbath. At six o'clock he listened to one more appeal from defense counsel covering the same matters he had heard before. A few minutes later he learned that President Eisenhower had turned down a final Rosenberg plea for clemency. Before 8:30 o'clock, Kaufman got word from the United States marshal that Julius and Ethel Rosenberg were dead.

A short while ago, John Knox, chief judge of the District Court, who had assigned the Rosenberg trial to Judge Kaufman two years before, looked thoughtfully out the window of his chambers, above bustling Foley Square. "There's never been pressure like this on our courts," he said. "It's more than that; it's closer to terror. But the courts must withstand such things or we would close the doors to justice and government.

"Now the good judge," he went on, "can only make his decisions within the limits of his finite mind and heart, using the best talents he has. Sometimes, as in such a case as this, the demands of decision are almost volcanic. The pressures keep building up inside you, and you must somehow resolve them. But in every volcano, you know, there's always an angle of repose. It comes when all energy is spent, all turbulence is over and nature has restored its balance."

CHAPTER 3

Affirming That Conscientious Objectors Must Oppose All War

Case Overview

Gillette v. United States (1971)

There have always been people with objections of conscience to war. Until the twentieth century, there was no U.S. law granting them legal status, although there were various ways of avoiding military service. During World War I, conscientious objector (CO) status was granted to members of religious sects that had a long history of pacifism, such as the Quakers and Mennonites. The law was broadened later to include anyone who objected on the basis of "religious training and belief" and, still later, to those whose moral objection was based solely on conscience rather than on religion. But always, CO status has required unwillingness to fight in *any* war, not just a particular war. People who would fight if the United States were directly attacked but not otherwise, for example, do not qualify.

During World War II this was not a large problem. The public supported that war, and most young men were willing and even eager to fight in it. The conscientious objectors were indeed men who believed it was wrong to kill under any circumstances. The Vietnam War, however, was different. Many people believed that the war was not justified, and large numbers of men resisted being drafted. Often this was a political objection rather than a conscientious one; some of these men moved to Canada, while others simply tried to evade the draft. Some even went to prison in order to make a political statement. However, there were also men whose objection to fighting in Vietnam was based entirely on conscience and who believed they had as much right to be classed as COs as those who could honestly declare that they would never fight in "war in any form," as the law requires.

Guy Porter Gillette was one of these men. He refused to be drafted and was sentenced to two years in prison. He would not tell the draft board that he would never fight in any war, he said in a *Life* magazine interview prior to the Supreme Court decision in his case. "I could easily have said that. Or I could have feigned illness or homosexuality. But if, in America, you have to lie to your government, I won't. There are wars I might fight in. I might fight if this country was attacked."

Louis Negre allowed himself to be drafted and went through basic training because he wanted to know all the facts and be really sure of his convictions before taking a stand. The training with bayonets and guns made him realize that he would not be willing to kill in a war he believed was unjust. When his application for conscientious objector status was denied, he was forced to go to Vietnam, but while there he did not have to fight. "They wanted to put me in ammunitions," he said in an interview for the Catholic Peace Fellowship. "I said that if I have to directly contribute to this war, I simply will refuse. And they accommodated me fairly decently; I did not have to carry a weapon and I worked a supply job." His case did not reach the Supreme Court until a year after he was discharged.

These two cases were combined when the Supreme Court agreed to review them, although the short title of its case includes only Gillette's name. The sincerity of the men's claims was not questioned; they were acknowledged to truly believe that it would be morally wrong to fight in Vietnam. Their lawyers argued that denying them CO status was in effect a violation of religious freedom because members of religions that opposed all war were exempt from fighting while people whose religious beliefs required opposition only to some wars were not. This argument was rejected by the Court, which maintained that the law was neutral with regard to religion and was not intended to discriminate, since it had valid secular purposes.

The Court held that exempting men from fighting in particular wars would make it impossible to administer the draft law fairly and would lower the morale of the armed forces. Some people doubted this, pointing out that the genuineness of potential COs' beliefs had to be individually investigated anyway. If Gillette and Negre had won their cases, however, there would have undoubtedly been a great many more applications for CO deferments, as the Vietnam War was widely thought to be unjust. It might indeed have made it harder for the government to raise an army.

The law, and the Supreme Court ruling in *Gillette v. United States*, still stand; they govern the granting of CO status to members of the armed forces today.

> "Persons who object solely to participa-
> tion in a particular war are not within
> the purview of the exempting section
> [of the law]."

Majority Opinion: The First Amendment Does Not Require Exemption of Selective Conscientious Objectors

Thurgood Marshall

Thurgood Marshall was the first African American to serve as a justice of the Supreme Court. In the following opinion in the combined cases of Gillette v. United States *and* Negre v. Larsen, *he first points out that the law unambiguously states that conscientious objectors must oppose all war in any form rather than just particular wars. He then considers the question of whether this law is an unconstitutional violation of religious freedom and concludes that it is not, since it is neutral with respect to religions and does not favor one over another. Finally, he states that the law has valid purposes having nothing to do with religion and that to allow exemption on the grounds of objection to particular wars would not be fair; therefore, the law as written is justifiable.*

These cases present the question whether conscientious objection to a particular war, rather than objection to war as such, relieves the objector from responsibilities of military

Thurgood Marshall, majority opinion, *Guy Porter Gillette v. United States* and *Louis A. Negre v. Stanley R. Larsen et al.*, U. S. Supreme Court, March 8, 1971. Reproduced by permission.

training and service. Specifically, we are called upon to decide whether conscientious scruples relating to a particular conflict are within the purview of established provisions relieving conscientious objectors to war from military service. Both petitioners also invoke constitutional principles barring government interference with the exercise of religion and requiring governmental neutrality in matters of religion.

In No. 85, petitioner [Guy] Gillette was convicted of willful failure to report for induction into the armed forces. Gillette defended on the ground that he should have been ruled exempt from induction as a conscientious objector to war. In support of his unsuccessful request for classification as a conscientious objector, this petitioner had stated his willingness to participate in a war of national defense or a war sponsored by the United Nations as a peace-keeping measure, but declared his opposition to American military operations in Vietnam, which he characterized as 'unjust.' Petitioner concluded that he could not in conscience enter and serve in the armed forces during the period of the Vietnam conflict. Gillette's view of his duty to abstain from any involvement in a war seen as unjust is, in his words, 'based on a humanist approach to religion,' and his personal decision concerning military service was guided by fundamental principles of conscience and deeply held views about the purpose and obligation of human existence.

The District Court determined that there was a basis in fact to support administrative denial of exemption in Gillette's case. The denial of exemption was upheld, and Gillette's defense to the criminal charge rejected, not because of doubt about the sincerity or the religious character of petitioner's objection to military service but because his objection ran to a particular war. In affirming the conviction, the Court of Appeals concluded that Gillette's conscientious beliefs 'were specifically directed against the war in Vietnam,' while the relevant exemption provision of the Military Selective Service Act of 1967, 'requires opposition 'to participation in war in any form."

In No. 325, petitioner [Louis] Negre, after induction into the Army, completion of basic training, and receipt of orders for Vietnam duty commenced proceedings looking to his discharge as a conscientious objector to war. Application for discharge was denied, and Negre sought judicial relief by habeas corpus. The District Court found a basis in fact for the Army's rejection of petitioner's application for discharge. Habeas relief was denied, and the denial was affirmed on appeal, because, in the language of the Court of Appeals, Negre 'objects to the war in Vietnam, not to all wars,' and therefore does 'not qualify for separation (from the Army), as a conscientious objector.' Again, no question is raised as to the sincerity or the religious quality of this petitioner's views.

We granted certiorari [review] in these cases, in order to resolve vital issues concerning the exercise of congressional power to raise and support armies, as affected by the religious guarantees of the First Amendment. We affirm the judgments below in both cases.

Must Oppose All War

Each petitioner claims a nonconstitutional right to be relieved of the duty of military service in virtue of his conscientious scruples. Both claims turn on the proper construction of section 6(j) of the Military Selective Service Act of 1967, which provides: 'Nothing contained in this title shall be construed to require any person to be subject to combatant training and service in the armed forces of the United States who, by reason of religious training and belief, is conscientiously opposed to participation in war in any form.' ...

For purposes of determining the statutory status of conscientious objection to a particular war, the focal language of section 6(j) is the phrase, 'conscientiously opposed to participation in war in any form.' This language, on a straightforward reading, can bear but one meaning; that conscientious scruples relating to war and military service must amount to conscientious opposition to participating personally in any war and all war. . . .

A different result cannot be supported by reliance on the materials of legislative history. Petitioners and amici point to no episode or pronouncement in the legislative history of section 6(j), or of predecessor provisions, that tends to overthrow the obvious interpretation of the words themselves.

It is true that the legislative materials reveal a deep concern for the situation of conscientious objectors to war, who absent special status would be put to a hard choice between contravening imperatives of religion and conscience or suffering penalties. Moreover, there are clear indications that congressional reluctance to impose such a choice stems from a recognition of the value of conscientious action to the democratic community at large, and from respect for the general proposition that fundamental principles of conscience and religious duty may sometimes override the demands of the secular state. But there are countervailing considerations, which are also the concern of Congress, and the legislative materials simply do not support the view that Congress intended to recognize any conscientious claim whatever as a basis for relieving the claimant from the general responsibility or the various incidents of military service. The claim that is recognized by section 6(j) is a claim of conscience running against war as such. This claim, not one involving opposition to a particular war only, was plainly the focus of congressional concern. . . .

It should be emphasized that our cases explicating the 'religious training and belief' clause of section 6(j), or cognate clauses of predecessor provisions, are not relevant to the present issue. The question here is not whether these petitioners' beliefs concerning war are 'religious' in nature. . . .

Nor do we decide that conscientious objection to a particular war necessarily falls within section 6(j)'s expressly excluded class of 'essentially political, sociological, or philosophical views, or a merely personal moral code.' Rather, we hold that Congress intended to exempt persons who oppose participating in all war—'participation in war in any form'—and that persons who object solely to participation in a particular war are not within the purview of the exempting section, even though the latter objection may have such roots in a claimant's conscience and personality that it is 'religious' in character. . . .

No Violation of Religious Freedom

Both petitioners argue that section 6[j], construed to cover only objectors to all war, violates the religious clauses of the First Amendment. The First Amendment provides that 'Congress shall make no law respecting an establishment of religion, or prohibiting the free exercise thereof.' Petitioners contend that Congress interferes with free exercise of religion by failing to relieve objectors to a particular war from military service, when the objection is religious or conscientious in nature. While the two religious clauses—pertaining to 'free exercise' and 'establishment' of religion—overlap and interact in many ways, it is best to focus first on petitioners' other contention, that section 6(j) is a law respecting the establishment of religion. For despite free exercise overtones, the gist of the constitutional complaint is that section 6(j) impermissibly discriminates among types of religious belief and affiliation.

On the assumption that these petitioners' beliefs concerning war have roots that are 'religious' in nature within the meaning of the Amendment as well as this Court's decisions construing section 6(j), petitioners ask how their claims to relief from military service can be permitted to fail, while other 'religious' claims are upheld by the Act. It is a fact that section 6(j), properly construed, has this effect. Yet we cannot conclude in mechanical fashion, or at all, that the section works an establishment of religion. . . .

The critical weakness of petitioners' establishment claim arises from the fact that section 6(j), on its face, simply does not discriminate on the basis of religious affiliation or religious belief, apart of course from beliefs concerning war. The section says that anyone who is conscientiously opposed to all war shall be relieved of military service. The specified objection must have a grounding in 'religious training and belief,' but no particular sectarian affiliation or theological position is required. The Draft Act of 1917 extended relief only to those conscientious objectors affiliated with some 'well-recognized religious sect or organization whose principles forbade members participation in war, but the attempt to focus on particular sects apparently broke down in administrative practice, and the 1940 Selective Training and Service Act discarded all sectarian restriction. Thereafter Congress has framed the conscientious objector exemption in broad terms compatible with 'its long-established policy of not picking and choosing among religious beliefs.' *United States v. Seeger.* . . .

Petitioners' contention is that the special statutory status accorded conscientious objection to all war, but not objection to a particular war, works a de facto discrimination among religions. This happens, say petitioners, because some religious faiths themselves distinguish between personal participation in 'just' and in 'unjust' wars, commending the former and forbidding the latter, and therefore adherents of some religious faiths—and individuals whose personal beliefs of a religious nature include the distinction—cannot object to all wars consistently with what is regarded as the true imperative of conscience. Of course, this contention of de facto religious discrimination, rendering § 6(j) fatally underinclusive, cannot simply be brushed aside. The question of governmental neutrality is not concluded by the observation that § 6(j) on its face makes no discrimination between religions, for the Establishment Clause forbids subtle departures from neutrality, 're-ligious gerrymanders,' as well as obvious abuses. Still a claim-ant alleging 'gerrymander' must be able to show the absence of a neutral, secular basis for the lines government has drawn. . . .

Valid Secular Purposes

Section 6[j] serves a number of valid purposes having nothing to do with a design to foster or favor any sect, religion, or cluster of religions. There are considerations of a pragmatic nature, such as the hopelessness of converting a sincere con-scientious objector into an effective fighting man, but no doubt the section reflects as well the view that 'in the forum of conscience, duty to a moral power higher than the state has always been maintained.' *United States v. Macintosh.* We have noted that the legislative materials show congressional con-cern for the hard choice that conscription would impose on conscientious objectors to war, as well as respect for the value of conscientious action and for the principle of supremacy of conscience.

Naturally the considerations just mentioned are affirma-tive in character, going to support the existence of an exemp-tion rather than its restriction specifically to persons who ob-ject to all war. The point is that these affirmative purposes are neutral in the sense of the Establishment Clause. . . .

'Neutrality' in matters of religion is not inconsistent with 'benevolence' by way of exemptions from onerous duties, so long as an exemption is tailored broadly enough that it re-flects valid secular purposes. In the draft area for 30 years the exempting provision has focused on individual conscientious belief, not on sectarian affiliation. The relevant individual be-lief is simply objection to all war, not adherence to any extra-neous theological viewpoint. And while the objection must have roots in conscience and personality that are 'religious' in nature, this requirement has never been construed to elevate conventional piety or religiosity of any kind above the imperatives of a personal faith.

In this state of affairs it is impossible to say that § 6(j) intrudes upon 'voluntarism' in religious life, or that the congressional purpose in enacting section 6(j) is to promote or foster those religious organizations that traditionally have taught the duty to abstain from participation in any war. A claimant, seeking judicial protection for his own conscientious beliefs, would be hard put to argue that section 6(j) encourages membership in putatively 'favored' religious organizations, for the painful dilemma of the sincere conscientious objector arises precisely because he feels himself bound in conscience not to compromise his beliefs or affiliations.

Unfair Determination

We conclude not only that the affirmative purposes underlying section 6(j) are neutral and secular, but also that valid neutral reasons exist for limiting the exemption to objectors to all war, and that the section therefore cannot be said to reflect a religious preference.

Apart from the Government's need for manpower, perhaps the central interest involved in the administration of conscription laws is the interest in maintaining a fair system for determining 'who serves when not all serve.' When the Government exacts so much, the importance of fair, evenhanded, and uniform decisionmaking is obviously intensified. The Government argues that the interest in fairness would be jeopardized by expansion of section 6(j) to include conscientious objection to a particular war. The contention is that the claim to relief on account of such objection is intrinsically a claim of uncertain dimensions, and that granting the claim in theory would involve a real danger of erratic or even discriminatory decisionmaking in administrative practice.

A virtually limitless variety of beliefs are subsumable under the rubric, 'objection to a particular war.' All the factors that might go into nonconscientious dissent from policy, also might appear as the concrete basis of an objection that has roots as well in conscience and religion. Indeed, over the realm of possible situations, opposition to a particular war may more likely be political and nonconscientious, than otherwise. The difficulties of sorting the two, with a sure hand, are considerable. Moreover, the belief that a particular war at a particular time is unjust is by its nature changeable and subject to nullification by changing events. Since objection may fasten on any of an enormous number of variables, the claim is ultimately subjective, depending on the claimant's view of the facts in relation to his judgment that a given factor or congeries of factors colors the character of the war as a whole. In short, it is not at all obvious in theory what sorts of objections should be deemed sufficient to excuse an objector, and there is considerable force in the Government's contention that a program of excusing objectors to particular wars may be 'impossible to conduct with any hope of reaching fair and consistent results.'

For their part, petitioners make no attempt to provide a careful definition of the claim to exemption that they ask the courts to carve out and protect. They do not explain why objection to a particular conflict—much less an objection that focuses on a particular facet of a conflict—should excuse the objector from all military service whatever, even from military operations that are connected with the conflict at hand in remote or tenuous ways. They suggest no solution to the problems arising from the fact that altered circumstances may quickly render the objection to military service moot. . . .

Ours is a Nation of enormous heterogeneity in respect of political views, moral codes, and religious persuasions. It does not bespeak an establishing of religion for Congress to forgo the enterprise of distinguishing those whose dissent has some conscientious basis from those who simply dissent. There is a danger that as between two would-be objectors, both having the same complaint against a war, that objector would succeed who is more articulate, better educated, or better counseled. There is even a danger of unintended religious discrimination—a danger that a claim's chances of success would be greater the more familiar or salient the claim's connection with conventional religiosity could be made to appear. At any rate, it is true that 'the more discriminating and complicated the basis of classification for an exemption—even a neutral one—the greater the potential for state involvement' in determining the character of persons' beliefs and affiliations, thus 'entangl(ing) government in difficult classifications of what is or is not religious,' or what is or is not conscientious. *Walz v. Tax Commission.* While the danger of erratic decisionmaking unfortunately exists in any system of conscription that takes individual differences into account, no doubt the dangers would be enhanced if a conscientious objection of indeterminate scope were honored in theory. . . .

It is not inconsistent with orderly democratic government for individuals to be exempted by law, on account of special characteristics, from general duties of a burdensome nature. But real dangers . . . might arise if an exemption were made available that in its nature could not be administered fairly and uniformly over the run of relevant fact situations. Should it be thought that those who go to war are chosen unfairly or capriciously, then a mood of bitterness and cynicism might corrode the spirit of public service and the values of willing performance of a citizen's duties that are the very heart of free government. . . .

We conclude that it is supportable for Congress to have decided that the objector to all war—to all killing in war—has a claim that is distinct enough and intense enough to justify special status, while the objector to a particular war does not.

Of course, we do not suggest that Congress would have acted irrationally or unreasonably had it decided to exempt those who object to particular wars. Our analysis of the policies of section 6(j) is undertaken in order to determine the existence vel non ["or not"] of a neutral, secular justification for the lines Congress has drawn. We find that justifying reasons exist and therefore hold that the Establishment Clause is not violated.

> "Conscience and belief are the main in-
> gredients of First Amendment rights."

Dissenting Opinion: Under the First Amendment, Individual Conscience Must Be Respected

William O. Douglas

William O. Douglas, who was a member of the Supreme Court from 1936 to 1975, was the longest-serving justice in Court history. He was a strong civil libertarian and supporter of First Amendment rights. The following is his dissenting opinion in the case of Gillette v. United States, *which also covered the case of Louis Negre. Douglas does not agree with the Court's ruling that distinguishing conscientious objectors to particular wars from objectors to all war does not violate religious freedom. In his opinion, the case is comparable to earlier ones in which the Court recognized that ethical values are as sincere and profound as those based on religion. Although the law excluding objectors to particular wars from conscientious objector status contains no explicit discrimination between religions, it is conscience, not religious affiliation, that is the true basis of First Amendment rights, he argues, and some people's consciences, as well as some formal religions, forbid participation in wars believed to be unjust. Therefore freedom of religion means that no one should be required to go against his or her conscience.*

William O. Douglas, dissenting opinion, *Guy Porter Gillette v. United States* and *Louis A. Negre v. Stanley R. Larsen et al.*, U. S. Supreme Court, March 8, 1971. Reproduced by permission.

[Guy Porter's] objection is to combat service in the Vietnam war, not to wars in general, and the basis of his objection is his conscience. His objection does not put him into the statutory exemption which extends to one 'who, by reason of religious training and belief, is conscientiously opposed to participation in war in any form.'

He stated his views as follows:

> I object to any assignment in the United States Armed Forces while this unnecessary and unjust war is being waged, on the grounds of religious belief specifically 'Humanism.' This essentially means respect and love for man, faith in his inherent goodness and perfectability, and confidence in his capability to improve some of the pains of the human condition.

This position is substantially the same as that of [Carl] Sisson in *United States v. Sisson*, where the District Court summarized the draftee's position as follows:

> Sisson's table of ultimate values is moral and ethical. It reflects quite as real, pervasive, durable, and commendable a marshalling of priorities as a formal religion. It is just as much a residue of culture, early training, and beliefs shared by companions and family. What another derives from the discipline of a church, Sisson derives from the discipline of conscience.

There is no doubt that the views of Gillette are sincere, genuine, and profound. The District Court in the present case faced squarely the issue presented in *Sisson* and being unable to distinguish the case on the facts, refused to follow *Sisson*.

The question, Can a conscientious objector, whether his objection be rooted in 'religion' or in moral values, be required to kill? has never been answered by the Court. *Hamilton v. Regents of University of California*, did no more than hold that the Fourteenth Amendment did not require a State to make its university available to one who would not take

military training. *United States v. Macintosh*, denied naturalization to a person who 'would not promise in advance to
bear arms in defense of the United States unless he believed
the war to be morally justified.' The question of compelling a
man to kill against his conscience was not squarely involved.
Most of the talk in the majority opinion concerned 'serving in
the armed forces of the nation in time of war.' Such service
can, of course, take place in noncombatant roles. The ruling
was that such service is 'dependent upon the will of Congress
and not upon the scruples of the individual, except as Congress provides.' The dicta of the Court in the Macintosh case
squint towards the denial of Gillette's claim, though as I have
said, the issue was not squarely presented.

Yet if dicta are to be our guide, my choice is the dicta of
Chief Justice [Charles Evans] Hughes who, dissenting in *Ma-
cintosh*, spoke as well for Justices [Oliver Wendell] Holmes,
[Louis] Brandeis, and [Harlan] Stone:

First Amendment Right of Conscience

Nor is there ground, in my opinion, for the exclusion of
Professor Macintosh because his conscientious scruples have
particular reference to wars believed to be unjust. There is
nothing new in such an attitude. Among the most eminent
statesmen here and abroad have been those who condemned
the action of their country in entering into wars they
thought to be unjustified. Agreements for the renunciation
of war presuppose a preponderant public sentiment against
wars of aggression. If, while recognizing the power of Congress, the mere holding of religious or conscientious scruples
against all wars should not disqualify a citizen from holding
office in this country, or an applicant otherwise qualified
from being admitted to citizenship, there would seem to be
no reason why a reservation of religious or conscientious
objection to participation in wars believed to be unjust
should constitute such a disqualification.

I think the Hughes view is the constitutional view. It is true that the First Amendment speaks of the free exercise of religion, not of the free exercise of conscience or belief. Yet conscience and belief are the main ingredients of First Amendment rights. They are the bedrock of free speech as well as religion. The implied First Amendment right of 'conscience' is certainly as high as the 'right of association' which we recognized *Shelton v. Tucker* and *NAACP v. Alabama*. Some indeed have thought it higher.

Conscience is often the echo of religious faith. But, as this case illustrates, it may also be the product of travail, meditation, or sudden revelation related to a moral comprehension of the dimensions of a problem, not to a religion in the ordinary sense.

[Novelist Leo] Tolstoy wrote of a man, one Van der Veer, 'who, as he himself says, is not a Christian, and who refuses military service, not from religious motives, but from motives of the simplest kind, motives intelligible and common to all men, of whatever religion or nation, whether Catholic, Mohammedan, Buddhist, Confucian, whether Spaniards or Japanese.

Van der Veer refuses military service, not because he follows the commandment. 'Thou shalt do no murder,' not because he is a Christian, but because he holds murder to be opposed to human nature.' Tolstoy goes on to say:

> Van der Veer says he is not a Christian. But the motives of his refusal and action are Christian. He refuses because he does not wish to kill a brother man; he does not obey, because the commands of his conscience are more binding upon him than the commands of men. . . . Thereby he shows that Christianity is not a sect or creed which some may profess and others reject; but that it is naught else than a life's following of that light of reason which illumines all men. . . .

> Those men who now behave rightly and reasonably do so, not because they follow prescriptions of Christ, but because

that line of action which was pointed out eighteen hundred years ago has now become identified with human conscience.

Duty to a Moral Power

The 'sphere of intellect and spirit,' as we described the domain of the First Amendment in *West Virginia State Board of Education v. Barnette*, was recognized [in] *United States v. Seeger*, where we gave a broad construction to the statutory exemption of those who by their religious training or belief are conscientiously opposed to participation in war in any form. We said: 'A sincere and meaningful belief which occupies in the life of its possessor a place parallel to that filled by the God of those admittedly qualifying for the exemption comes within the statutory definition.'

Seeger does not answer the present question as Gillette is not 'opposed to participation in war in any form.'

But the constitutional infirmity in the present Act seems obvious once 'conscience' is the guide. As Chief Justice Hughes said in the Macintosh case:

> But, in the forum of conscience, duty to a moral power higher than the state has always been maintained. The reservation of that supreme obligation, as a matter of principle, would unquestionably be made by many of our conscientious and law-abiding citizens. The essence of religion is belief in a relation to God involving duties superior to those arising from any human relation.'

The law as written is a species of those which show an invidious discrimination in favor of religious persons and against others with like scruples. Mr. Justice [Hugo] Black once said: 'The First Amendment has lost much if the religious follower and the atheist are no longer to be judicially regarded as entitled to equal justice under law.' *Zorach v. Clauson*. We said as much in our recent decision *Epperson v.*

Arkansas, where we struck down as unconstitutional a state law prohibiting the teaching of the doctrine of evolution in the public schools:

> Government in our democracy, state and national, must be neutral in matters of religious theory, doctrine, and practice. It may not be hostile to any religion or to the advocacy of no-religion; and it may not aid, foster, or promote one religion or religious theory against another or even against the militant opposite. The First Amendment mandates governmental neutrality between religion and religion, and between religion and nonreligion.

While there is no Equal Protection Clause in the Fifth Amendment, our decisions are clear that invidious classifications violate due process. *Bolling v. Sharpe*, held that segregation by race in the public schools was an invidious discrimination, and *Schneider v. Rusk*, reached the same result based on penalties imposed on naturalized, not native-born citizens. A classification of 'conscience' based on a 'religion' and a 'conscience' based on more generalized, philosophical grounds is equally invidious by reason of our First Amendment standards.

I had assumed that the welfare of the single human soul was the ultimate test of the vitality of the First Amendment.

This is an appropriate occasion to give content to our dictum in *West Virginia State Board of Education v. Barnette*. '(F)reedom to differ is not limited to things that do not matter much. . . . The test of its substance is the right to differ as to things that touch the heart of the existing order.'

I would reverse this judgment.

The Case of Louis Negre

I approach the facts of [the Negre] case with some diffidence, as they involve doctrines of the Catholic Church in which I was not raised. But we have on one of petitioner's briefs an authoritative lay Catholic scholar, Dr. John T. Noonan, Jr., and from that brief I deduce the following:

Under the doctrines of the Catholic Church a person has a moral duty to take part in wars declared by his government so long as they comply with the tests of his church for just wars. Conversely, a Catholic has a moral duty not to participate in unjust wars.

The Fifth Commandment, 'Thou shall not kill,' provides a basis for the distinction between just and unjust wars. In the 16th century Francisco Victoria, Dominican master of the University of Salamanca and pioneer in international law, elaborated on the distinction. 'If a subject is convinced of the injustice of a war, he ought not to serve in it, even on the command of his prince. This is clear, for no one can authorize the killing of an innocent person.' He realized not all men had the information of the prince and his counsellors on the causes of a war, but where 'the proofs and tokens of the injustice of the war may be such that ignorance would be no excuse even to the subjects' who are not normally informed, that ignorance will not be an excuse if they participate. Well over 400 years later, today, the Baltimore Catechism makes an exception to the Fifth Commandment for a 'soldier fighting in a just war.'

No one can tell a Catholic that this or that war is either just or unjust. This is a personal decision that an individual must make on the basis of his own conscience after studying the facts.

Like the distinction between just and unjust wars, the duty to obey conscience is not a new doctrine in the Catholic Church. When told to stop preaching by the Sanhedrin, to which they were subordinate by law, 'Peter and the apostles answered and said, 'We must obey God rather than men.'' That duty has not changed. Pope Paul VI has expressed it as follows; 'On his part, man perceives and acknowledges the imperatives of the divine law through the mediation of conscience. In all his activity a man is bound to follow his conscience, in order that he may come to God, the end and purpose of life.'

The Catholic View of Modern Warfare

While the fact that the ultimate determination of whether a war is unjust rests on individual conscience, the Church has provided guides. Francisco Victoria referred to 'killing of an innocent person.' World War II had its impact on the doctrine. Writing shortly after the war Cardinal Ottaviani stated: '(M)odern wars can never fulfil those conditions which (as we stated earlier on in this essay) govern—theoretically—a just and lawful war. Moreover, no conceivable cause could ever be sufficient justification for the evils, the slaughter, the destruction, the moral and religious upheavals which war today entails. In practice, then, a declaration of war will never be justifiable.' The full impact of the horrors of modern war were emphasized in the Pastoral Constitution announced by Vatican II:

> 'The development of armaments by modern science has immeasurably magnified the horrors and wickedness of war. Warfare conducted with these weapons can inflict immense and indiscriminate havoc which goes far beyond the bounds of legitimate defense. Indeed, if the kind of weapons now stocked in the arsenals of the great powers were to be employed to the fullest, the result would be the almost complete reciprocal slaughter of one side by the other, not to speak of the widespread devastation that would follow in the world and the deadly aftereffects resulting from the use of such arms.

> 'All these factors force us to undertake a completely fresh reappraisal of war.

> '(I)t is one thing to wage a war of self-defense; it is quite another to seek to impose domination on another nation.

The Pastoral Constitution announced that '(e)very act of war directed to the indiscriminate destruction of whole cities or vast areas with their inhabitants is a crime against God and man which merits firm and unequivocal condemnation.'

Negre's Convictions

Louis Negre is a devout Catholic. In 1951 when he was four, his family immigrated to this country from France. He attended Catholic schools in Bakersfield, California, until graduation from high school. Then he attended Bakersfied Junior College for two years. Following that, he was inducted into the Army.

At the time of his induction he had his own convictions about the Vietnam war and the Army's goals in the war. He wanted, however, to be sure of his convictions. 'I agreed to myself that before making any decision or taking any type of stand on the issue, I would permit myself to see and understand the Army's explanation of its reasons for violence in Vietnam. For, without getting an insight on the subject, it would be unfair for me to say anything, without really knowing the answer.'

On completion of his advanced infantry training, 'I knew that if I would permit myself to go to Vietnam I would be violating my own concepts of natural law and would be going against all that I had been taught in my religious training.' Negre applied for a discharge as a conscientious objector. His application was denied. He then refused to comply with an order to proceed for shipment to Vietnam. A general court-martial followed, but he was acquitted. After that he filed this application for discharge as a conscientious objector.

Negre is opposed under his religious training and beliefs to participation in any form in the war in Vietnam. His sincerity is not questioned. His application for a discharge, however, was denied because his religious training and beliefs led him to oppose only a particular war which according to his conscience was unjust.

For the reasons I have stated in my dissent in the Gillette case decided this day, I would reverse the judgment.

| *"Neither of the two governmental inter-ests weighed by the Supreme Court in* Gillette *would be seriously jeopardized should conscientious objector defer-ments be made available to selective objectors."*

Deferring Selective Conscientious Objectors Would Do No Harm to the Military

David Malament

David Malament is a professor of logic and the philosophy of science at the University of California, Irvine. During the Viet-nam War he was a conscientious objector and served time in prison for refusing induction into the military. The following viewpoint is a portion of an article he wrote while he was a graduate student. In it he argues that the Supreme Court's con-clusion in Gillette v. United States *that it is more difficult to de-termine the sincerity of conscientious objection to a particular war than to all war is not valid. In neither case will a claim of conscientious objection be accepted without evidence, so it is not true that it would be impossible to administer the draft laws fairly if all such objections were grounds for exemption from military service. Furthermore, he says, deferring all conscientious objectors would not cause morale in the military to be any lower than it already is. (During the Vietnam War, when this was written, it was extremely low.) In his opinion, since there are no real reasons why distinguishing types of conscientious objection increases military effectiveness, it is unconstitutional to do so.*

The Military Selective Service Act provides for the deferment, on condition of alternate civilian service, of those "who, by reason of religious training and belief, [are] conscientiously opposed to participation in war in any form." In recent years considerable effort has been devoted to the interpretation of this clause, and in particular to the question of whether objectors to a particular war, so-called selective conscientious objectors, may qualify for exemption. . . .

According to the *Gillette* [*v. United States*] decision, Congress reasonably assumed that serious governmental interests would be jeopardized if conscientious objection privileges were extended to selective objectors. I shall argue that it is not at all clear that this would be the case. The government makes several different claims to this effect, but all are questionable.

Two governmental interests are mentioned in the decision. The first is that of fair administrability. The government warned that a program excusing selective objectors would be "impossible to conduct with any hope of reaching fair and consistent results." It would "involve a real danger of erratic and even discriminatory decision-making in administrative practice." The second interest is that of maintaining the effectiveness and morale of our armed forces. . . .

The Court is concerned about the administrative difficulty of answering two questions: first, whether an objection is conscientious, and second, whether the objection is religious in the proper sense, rather than political. The Court seems to accept the claim that these determinations would not be merely more difficult to make in the case of selective objection, but so much more difficult that fair administration of the Selective Service Act would be impossible. In order to evaluate this claim, which is central to the Court's decision, it is necessary

to review how the Court has previously interpreted the first
two parts of the three-part test for eligibility as a conscientious objector.

Past Rules for Objector Status

The first federal conscription bill that made provision for conscientious objectors was enacted during World War I. It provided exemption only to members of historic peace churches,
such as Quakers and Mennonites. The next bill, in 1940, made
no mention of membership in a traditionally recognized religious organization, but provided exemption for those "who,
by reason of religious training and belief, [are] conscientiously
opposed to participation in war in any form." In 1948 a qualifying sentence was added: "Religious training and belief in
this connection means an individual's belief in a relation to a
Supreme Being involving duties superior to those arising from
any human relation, but does not include essentially political,
sociological, or philosophical views, or a merely personal
moral code."

The qualification was added to clarify matters, but it had
the opposite effect. In a series of cases the "Supreme Being"
test was challenged as being prejudicially narrow, since it excluded such religions as "secular humanism." The distinction
between religious beliefs and those stemming from a "personal
moral code" was also challenged as being vague, arbitrary, or
discriminatory.

The Supreme Court came to accept these challenges in the
[*United States v.*] *Seeger* decision in 1965. In his application
Seeger had refused either to affirm or deny belief in a Supreme Being. He had crossed out the words "training and" in
the phrase "religious training and belief" and put quotation
marks around "religious." The Court decided that he qualified
as a conscientious objector nevertheless. It formulated what
has become known as the "equivalency test" of religious belief.
What is required is "a sincere and meaningful belief which oc-

cupies in the life of the possessor a place parallel to that filled by the God of those admittedly qualifying for exemption."

In response to *Seeger* the Congress deleted the Supreme Being clause in 1967, but left the second half of the qualification, that religious training and belief "does not include essentially political, sociological, or philosophical views, or a merely personal moral code." The Selective Service Act was in that form when Gillette violated it and it has not been changed since.

In its decision in *Welsh* [*v. United States*] in 1970 the Court went further and interpreted away some of the force of the restrictive clause about merely personal moral codes. Welsh simply struck out the words "religious training and belief" when filling out his application and described himself as a humanist, much as Gillette did. The Court decided, nonetheless, that his position was religious in the proper sense and that he should not have been denied his classification. It applied the following test: "If an individual deeply and sincerely holds beliefs which are purely ethical or moral in source and content but which nevertheless impose upon him a duty of conscience to refrain from participating in any war at any time, he is entitled to deferment as a conscientious objector." As of the time it heard Gillette's appeal, this was the Court's criterion for eligibility as a conscientious objector. It reaffirmed this position in the course of its decision in *Gillette*. Thus if the Court is to distinguish political from religious objection, and contend further that selective objection is "likely to be political," it is bound to interpret religion in this sense, which does not exclude secular conscience.

Political vs. Conscientious Objection

What is the distinction? The Court never gives an example, but I assume it would consider political the following reasons for opposing a particular war: (a) the war is one of imperialist intervention; (b) it is contrary to the interests of the international working class; or (c) it is contrary to the national interest (of the country in whose army the objector is asked to fight). I further assume that it would have to consider an objection based on the Christian just war doctrine to be properly religious. . . .

I do not question that objections such as (a), (b), or (c) are in a good sense political in character. So are all normative judgments about the affairs of a national state, polls, or other body politic. The Christian doctrine that defines the conditions under which war is justified is itself political. But the sense in which these judgments are political is not incompatible with derivation from "religious training and belief" as the phrase is interpreted in *Seeger* and *Welsh,* or even in the most traditional interpretation. God might reveal his will concerning the affairs of state and command men to act accordingly. . . .

It should also be clear that normative principles concerning warfare which we traditionally associate with religious sects can be shared by nonbelievers. The Christian just war doctrine, which the Court must recognize as a possible religious foundation for selective objection, is not at all sectarian. Quite the contrary. Some of the principles of the doctrine have even been incorporated into the body of international law which defines the permissible circumstances and means of war. One might embrace the just war doctrine as the will of God as revealed in personal mystical communion or through the mediation of a long heritage of religious teachings. But one might also embrace its criteria within a different framework; as a secular moral intuitionist, as a contractarian, or as a utilitarian of one sort or another. And one might do so with such depth of conviction as to satisfy the Court's "equivalency test" that belief be religious.

Of course not every objection to war couched in political language need reflect deeply felt moral obligations or the dictates of conscience. But neither is this necessarily the case with objection couched in what the Court would probably consider religious language. In worrying about whether objection is political the Court is worrying about the wrong question.

The force of *Seeger* and *Welsh* was to collapse the condition that objection be based on religious training and belief into the condition that it be conscientious, i.e., that it be deeply and sincerely held and derive from the binding obligations of conscience, divinely inspired or not. The proper question for administrative determination is whether a draft-age opponent of a given war is conscientious in this sense.

Determining Sincerity

The government's central claim, accepted by the Court, is that this determination is harder to make when objection is framed with respect to a particular war than when it is framed with respect to all wars. The determination, in fact, is so difficult that a program excusing selective objectors would be "impossible to conduct with any hope of reaching fair and consistent results." I cannot see why it would be harder to conduct than the present program. I certainly cannot see why it would be "impossible" to conduct. And yet surely only insuperable administrative difficulty, not mere administrative inconvenience, is the sort of governmental interest which may be weighed against basic rights as guaranteed in the free exercise, nonestablishment, and equal protection clauses of the Constitution.

Admittedly, in individual cases it may be difficult to determine whether a would-be conscientious objector is truly conscientious. But in these cases the difficulty has nothing to do with whether his objection is particular or universal. There is a confusion here between the substance of a position relating to the justifiability of war and the sincerity of an applicant who claims to embrace the position on grounds of conscience. The fact that a man *claims* opposition to all wars is no proof that he qualifies for deferment. . . .

The Selective Service System does not accept claims to conscientious objection at face value. A personal statement, references, and an interview are required. The local draft boards have the responsibility for judging depth and sincerity of belief on the basis of this evidence. Decisions may be appealed and all determinations are subject to review in the federal courts. The mechanisms whereby we evaluate sincerity and intent are surely fallible and subjective, but they are not more so in the case of claims of selective objection than in those of universal objection. In fact a would-be selective objector, unlike his counterpart, may properly be held accountable for substantive information about the nature of the war he opposes. This might actually facilitate an evaluation of his conscientiousness. Furthermore, however imperfect our ability to judge states of mind, juries make such judgments every day in cases where intent or sincerity is a factor in the determination of guilt.

The Court elaborates upon the difficulty of processing would-be selective conscientious objectors by listing three specific worries. First, "an objector's claim to exemption might be based on some feature of a conflict which most would regard as incidental, or might be predicated on a view of the facts which most would regard as mistaken." . . .

It should be recognized that very few objectors, if any, would base their objection "on some feature of a conflict which most would regard as incidental." The overwhelming majority of draft-age opponents of the Vietnam War base their opposition on the belief that, at the very least, it is causing death, injury, destruction, and human misery completely out of proportion to any good that might come of it. These "features" are not incidental.

Neither does it seem especially significant that objection to a particular war might be "predicated on a view of the facts which most would regard as mistaken." As long as objectors to the war are in the minority this will surely be the case. But the majority, of course, may be wrong about the facts. . . . Even if we could say objectively that the majority view was correct, those who failed to recognize this might still be conscientious. Speaking to this very point, the Court held in *Seeger* that: "the 'truth' of a belief is not open to question"; rather, the question is whether the objector's beliefs are "truly held."

Second, the Court notes that "the belief that a particular war at a particular time is unjust is by its nature changeable and subject to nullification by changing events." . . .

Though objectors to particular wars, even when conscientious, may change their positions, it does not follow that they should not be deferred. Rather it follows that conscientious objector classifications should be subject to periodic review in precisely the way certain medical, occupational, and hardship deferments are. The Selective Service System manages to review these claims regularly even though their number dwarfs that of conscientious objection claims.

Third, the Court acknowledges the government's claim that expansion of exemption provisions would discriminate in favor of the "articulate, better educated, or better counseled." The proper response to this is the same as to the first and second difficulties outlined by the Court. Whatever advantage a well-counseled college graduate might have before his board he will have whether he tries to convince it of the conscientiousness of his objection to one war or to all wars. . . .

Effect of Deferments on the Military

The second substantial government interest mentioned by the Court in *Gillette* is that of maintaining the effectiveness and morale of our armed forces. If selective objectors were permitted to perform alternate civilian service or noncombatant military service, it is possible that there would not be enough men left to fill army quotas. Even if soldiers were available in sufficient numbers, some might resent the exemption of others, and this resentment would "weaken the resolve" required of fighting men. . . .

If so many men were conscientiously opposed to a given war that it became impossible to fill even a small quota, then it would be questionable whether the government was justified in going to war in the first place, or in using conscripts to do so. In fact, however, much to the disappointment of war opponents, the number of men conscientiously opposed to service in recent years has never been large enough to threaten army quotas. Volunteers have always been in the majority; their proportion might have been still larger if the army had raised its salaries and benefits, as it has done more recently. Furthermore, many of the men who might have been selective conscientious objectors qualified simultaneously for student or occupational deferments. . . .

Granted the problem is much more serious when a war is as unpopular as the [Vietnam] war and has produced so great a national polarization. There are undoubtedly large numbers of conscripts who are not prepared to declare themselves as conscientious objectors but who nevertheless serve only because they feel it their duty. They may have reservations about the justice or necessity of the war, or may simply be concerned about the inconvenience or danger involved in military service—quite rightly so. This reluctant conscript might well think it unfair that his more zealous neighbor, even if conscientious, is permitted alternate service or noncombatant military service. Once such a conscript is ordered to Vietnam, or when he first sees combat, he might well be resentful.

This objection could be directed to the deferment of universal objectors as well as to selective objectors, but not with the same force. Pacifists, like celibates perhaps, are considered odd but usually tolerable. The selective objector, however, presents a more focused dissent and may arouse greater anger. There is a difference between telling a businessman that all business is corrupt and telling him that a particular business practice in which he is engaged is dishonest.

A reluctant conscript may feel duty-bound to serve, but only if the onerous duty is shared fairly. His position is entirely justified. The question is whether *fairness* is compromised when the selective objector is permitted alternate service. . . .

It might be argued, however, that idealized considerations of fairness are irrelevant. Even if army morale *should* not be influenced by the deferment of selective objectors, in fact it might be. The government's concern, the argument repeats, must be considered against the bitter background of the Vietnam War and not against idealized models of political justice.

This sort of cynical realism deserves a response in kind. There *is* widespread bitterness in the army; morale is low, at times mutinously so. Soldiers returning from Vietnam tell stories of men refusing direct orders and shooting officers. Drug abuse is common. Men are deserting in large numbers. The Pentagon concedes that over 98,000 men deserted in 1971 and that over 350,000 have done so since 1967, when Gillette was denied his conscientious objector classification. Morale is probably as low as it has ever been. And the condition is certainly exacerbated by the presence within the army of vocal opponents of the war who express their feelings, turn out at newspapers, and organize open resistance. The center of the antiwar movement has in fact shifted from the college campuses to military bases on the one hand, and to the federal prisons on the other. The government, so concerned about morale, must weigh the disruption that might result from the quiet deferment of conscientious war opponents against the disruption that results even now from their presence in the army or from their conspicuous imprisonment. It is a grim utility calculation indeed.

If my argument is sound, neither of the two government interests weighed by the Supreme Court in *Gillette* would be seriously jeopardized should conscientious objector deferments be made available to selective objectors. These interests would be no more compromised than they are under the present system. In the absence of such overriding considerations it is unconstitutional to recognize one sort of religious objection to partipation in war but not another. Guy Gillette should not have been sent to prison.

"Opposition to a particular war can be every bit as 'conscientious' as opposition to war in any form."

Conscientious Objection Is No Less Strong When Selective than When General

G. Albert Ruesga

G. Albert Ruesga is a former professor of philosophy and now president and chief executive officer of the Greater New Orleans Foundation. In the following viewpoint he criticizes the Supreme Court's ruling in Gillette v. United States *that selective conscientious objectors (SCOs) are not exempt from military duty. He argues that the government's reasons for not exempting them apply just as much to those who oppose all war as to those who oppose only particular wars and that objection to fighting may be equally conscientious in both cases. Furthermore, he says, the Court drew a shaky line between political objections and conscientious objections, because the factors on which objection is based may involve both. In his opinion, as the Court itself made clear that draft boards should judge only whether a belief is truly held rather than the truth or falsity of the belief, it would be better to honor all types of conscientious objections than to distinguish among them.*

Although the character of recent U.S. military aggressions have obviated the need for a Vietnam War–style draft, the issue of conscientious objection is still very much with us and

G. Albert Ruesga, "Selective Conscientious Objection and the Right Not to Kill," *Social Theory and Practice*, Spring 1995, pp. 61–81. Copyright © 1995 by Social Theory and Practice. Reproduced by permission of the publisher and the author.

very much unresolved. Current [in the mid-1990s] policy is to grant an exemption from military service only to those whose conscientious scruples extend to *all* wars. The relevant section of the Military Service Act of 1967 reads as follows:

> Nothing contained in this title . . . shall be construed to require any person to be subject to combatant training and service in the armed forces of the United States who, by reason of religious training and belief, is conscientiously opposed to participation in war in any form.

A number of court cases have extended the meaning of the "religious training and belief" clause, but this exemption from military service continues to be denied to those who object to *particular* wars (as opposed to "war in any form"). This essay will focus on these so-called *selective* conscientious objectors (SCOs). . . .

Gillette v. United States

Current U.S. policy toward selective conscientious objectors is governed by the Supreme Court's ruling in *Gillette v. United States*. In this case, the petitioners challenged the constitutionality of section 6(j) of the Military Selective Service Act (quoted above) on the grounds that it violated the Free Exercise and Establishment of Religion clauses of the First Amendment. There can be little doubt that section 6(j) of the Selective Service Act benefits the adherents of some religious creeds and works to the detriment of others. The conscientious scruples of traditional pacifists, like the Quakers and Mennonites, for example, are protected by this law, while the particular misgivings of selective conscientious objectors are given no quarter. Justice [Thurgood] Marshall, who delivered the Court's ruling, freely admitted that section 6(j) indeed had the effect of "permitting" the petitioners' religious claims to exemption from military service to fail, while upholding the religious claims of other COs. Nevertheless, he argued that it was not possible to "conclude in mechanical fashion, or at all, that the section works an establishment of religion."

As against petitioners' claims that the Selective Service Act violates the Establishment Clause of the First Amendment, the Court concluded that

> There are valid, neutral reasons, with the central emphasis on the maintenance of fairness in the administration of military conscription, for the congressional limitation of the exemption to "war in any form," and [that] therefore section 6(j) cannot be said to reflect a religious preference.

I hope to convince the reader that the Court's reasons for rejecting the petitioners' claims serve equally well as grounds for rejecting *all* claims to CO status, including those presently protected by law. In arguing that the Selective Service Act does not violate the Establishment Clause, the Government must not simply show that "valid, neutral reasons" exist for military conscription per se, but rather that valid, neutral reasons exist for failing to extend the protection of section 6(j) to selective conscientious objectors. I will assume, as does the Court, that the need for military conscription can at times be established—especially in times of national emergency.

In support of its policy, the Government argues that

> interest in fairness would be jeopardized by expansion of §6(j) to include conscientious objection to a particular war. The contention is that the claim to relief on account of such objection is intrinsically *a claim of uncertain dimensions*, and that granting the claim in theory would involve a real danger of erratic or even discriminatory decision-making in administrative practice.

A fair assessment of the Government's position thus necessarily entails an evaluation of the arguments that seek to show that the danger of erratic or discriminatory decision-making in the administration of the Selective Service Act is *greater* in the case of SCOs than in the case of non-SCOs. The primary reason given by the Court for concluding that selective conscientious objection is a "claim of uncertain dimensions" is that

> A virtually limitless variety of beliefs are subsumable under the rubric "objection to a particular war." . . . Indeed over the realm of possible situations, opposition to a particular war may more likely be political and nonconscientious, than otherwise.

Claims May Be Just as Questionable

The Court argues, essentially, that the SCO's objection to serving in a particular war may be motivated in part or in whole by his "nonconscientious dissent" from government policy. The Selective Service Board would thus be put in the difficult position of having to categorize and assess the SCO's reasons for objecting to military service, rejecting those reasons that were not clearly conscientious in character. Suppose, for example, that the claimant objected to a particular war because he deemed that the government's purposes in waging the war were offensive rather than defensive. (We might assume that the SCO in question conscientiously rejects participation in any offensive war, but would consider participation in a purely defensive war.) The Selective Service Board in this case would then be required to determine whether or not the war in question was in fact being fought for offensive purposes—perhaps in the face of government claims to the contrary. Requiring draft boards to make these difficult judgments would ultimately result in an unfair or uneven administration of the Selective Service Act: a draft board that shared the SCO's political judgments would absolve him of military duty; a draft board that did not share his judgments would reject his claim to CO status.

While it is certainly true that the Government has an important interest in the fair administration of the Selective Service Act, and that the claims of SCOs may be problematic (in the manner just described), it is also clear that non-SCO claims to exemption from military service may be of equally "uncertain dimensions." Suppose, for example, that a non-SCO opposes war in any form because he believes that all wars are offensive wars. The Court does not appear to acknowledge the fact that this objection to war in any form may be every bit as "political and nonconscientious" as the objection of the SCO. While the non-SCO in question may oppose military service because he believes that all offensive wars are immoral (a clearly conscientious claim), he may nevertheless have come to the conclusion that all wars are offensive wars through some egregious failure of logic or common sense, or he may have been motivated by (nonconscientious) objections to American foreign policy decisions. According to Justice Marshall, however, "the relevant, individual belief is simply objection to *all* war," with the important proviso, of course, that one's opposition to all war be conscientious and rooted in religious training and belief. Denying an exemption to the SCO who claims that *this particular war* is an offensive war, and granting it to the non-SCO who claims that *all* wars are offensive wars, would thus appear to involve the draft board in a bizarre kind of logocentrism in which universal categorical propositions are favored over particular categorical propositions. And yet both the objections of the SCO and of the non-SCO would appear to rest on the same uncertainties of judgment. If it is true therefore that "a virtually limitless variety of beliefs are subsumable under the rubric, 'objection to a particular war,'" then it seems no less true that a limitless variety of beliefs are subsumable under the rubric "objection to all wars."

It may, of course, be possible for a draft board to challenge the premises of the conscript who believes, for example, that all wars are offensive wars, and who rejects military service on this basis. But it is far from clear that the draft board can proceed in this manner when the conscript's objections rest not on the authority of his own judgment, but on the authority of some religious creed to which he adheres. Suppose, for example, that the non-SCO belongs to a sect whose religious head proclaims the sect's opposition to all wars on the basis of false premises or on the basis of some other failure of logic or common sense. The sect in question may believe that all wars are immoral because they are financed by a secret cabal of international financiers, or they may believe that all wars waged by the U.S. government are waged to promote the interests of the wealthy—and there are many other possibilities. In these scenarios, the non-SCO's claim to exemption from military service should, according to the criteria laid down by the courts, be upheld: assuming that his claim is conscientious (that is, assuming that he did not join the sect in question simply to get out of military service), then there can be little doubt that his rejection of all wars is appropriately rooted in religious training and belief. Notice that here again we have the possibility of a limitless variety of beliefs subsumable under the rubric "opposition to war in any form"—beliefs that, because of their universal form ("*all* wars"), are fully protected by law.

A Shaky Line

Part of the problem with the Court's ruling in *Gillette v. United States* is the very shaky line it attempts to draw between conscientious dissent, on the one hand, and purely political dissent, on the other. We are warned that "[a]ll the factors that might go into nonconscientious dissent from policy, also might appear as the concrete basis of an objection that has roots as well in conscience and religion." But when is dissent from policy ever purely nonconscientious? And what would nonconscientious dissent from policy look like? The examples provided by the Court are revealing:

> A war may be thought "just" or not depending on one's assessment of these factors and many more: the character of the foe, or of allies; the place the war is fought; the likeli-

hood that a military clash will issue in benefits, of various kinds, enough to override the inevitable costs of conflict. And so on.

Thus, taking the first example in the passage, the SCO might believe that a particular war is unjust because he is convinced that the enemy is outnumbered ten to one, and his moral scruples will not allow him to participate in a "war" that will amount to little more than a massacre. We may even assume that there are Government troop estimates that contradict the SCO's judgment. By calling the SCO's objection "nonconscientious," however, we fail to appreciate the *moral* dimension of his choosing to believe a proposition p even in the face of evidence that p is false. The conscript in our scenario may choose to reject the evidence provided by the Government because he believes that troop estimates have been mistaken in the past, and that the prescription against participating in a massacre outweighs the possibility that the Government's estimate may now be accurate. He may, for other reasons, simply mistrust the Government. These and other decisions may ultimately involve the SCO in a failure of reason, or of good sense, but cannot the same can be said for the traditional pacifist who believes that all wars are immoral, and who can provide little concrete evidence that this is in fact the case?

In the majority ruling in *Gillette v. United States*, the Court pointed out that the "petitioners [made] no attempt to provide a careful definition of the claim to exemption that they [asked] the courts to carve out and protect." If the Court wished to spare conscripts the "danger of erratic or even discriminatory decision-making" in the administration of the Selective Service Act, one solution would have been to require draft boards to honor *all* conscientious claims to exemption from military service. After all, the Court made it clear that draft boards should not be in the business of judging the truth or falsity of beliefs held by conscripts, "the question is whether the objector's beliefs are 'truly held.'" And it appears that opposition to a particular war can be every bit as "conscientious" as opposition to war in any form, and that the premises on which this opposition is based can be just as "truly held" as any others.

I do not here wish to assess the utilitarian-style arguments that have been made both for and against this proposal, in part because I believe that these arguments are difficult, if not impossible, to assess. I refer the reader to David Malament's excellent discussion of these issues [included in this chapter of the present volume]. I do believe, however, that the implementation of this proposal would have a number of welcome effects. For example, in order to guarantee an adequate number of troops for a given campaign, the Government would be required to make a stronger case for military deployment than it does at present. And this, I assume, would be a boon to any democracy worthy of the name. . . .

More Difficult Moral Decisions

Harlan Fiske Stone, who later became Chief Justice, once wrote that

> both morals and sound policy require that the state should not violate the conscience of the individual. All our history gives confirmation to the view that liberty of conscience has a moral and social value which makes it worthy of preservation at the hands of the state. So deep in its significance and vital, indeed, is it to the integrity of man's moral and spiritual nature that nothing short of the self-preservation of the state should warrant its violation; and it may well be questioned whether the state which preserves its life by a settled policy of violation of the conscience of the individual will not in fact ultimately lose it by the process.

The Court has again and again reaffirmed the State's regard for individual conscience, even when this regard for conscience required some sacrifice in social utility. This same respect for the forum of conscience can be observed in the provision made in section 6(j) of the Selective Service Act for those who conscientiously oppose war in any form. But does Congress's unwillingness to extend this protection to *selective* conscientious objectors reflect, perhaps, some hidden assumptions about the SCO's commitment to the principle that one should not kill? Does the SCO's willingness to participate in *some* wars, for example, reflect less of a commitment on his part to the preservation of human life? The answer is that it would if we could assume that the preservation of human life entailed little more than refraining from killing. But of course we cannot make this assumption. The SCO will often believe that the preservation of some lives can only be purchased at the cost of others. To reason thus, to make what many SCOs see as a regrettable choice, does not in any way signal a weak regard for the sanctity of human life. The SCO's willingness to take up arms in some cases does not indicate that the demands of his conscience are any less stringent or binding. The pacifist who adheres to the principle that all wars are immoral avoids the often painful exercise of conscience experienced by those who must find a way to balance conflicting principles. If the law honors the conscientious scruples of pacifists in virtue of their conscientiousness, then justice demands that it do the same for those who must bear the assaults of a moral dilemma and somehow resolve the conflicting demands of conscience. . . .

We venerate those war heroes who show tenacity and courage on the battlefield. We do not, as far as I can tell, applaud those soldiers who clearly intuit the barbarism of a given war and who refuse to take up arms. We have yet to understand the heroic dimensions of the SCO's refusing to participate in a war that he clearly perceives to be unjust. . . .

To deny the validity and strength of these claims is to discourage individual citizens from making moral assessments of public policy. There is no doubt a danger in allowing individuals to choose which laws they will obey and which they will disobey; there is indeed a sense in which we delegate a certain amount of responsibility for public policy decisions to our elected representatives. But I do not believe that this delegation of responsibility entails that we should honor public policy decisions that so profoundly abrogate the dictates of individual conscience.

Conscientious Objectors Must Use Practical Reasoning to Resolve the Conflict Between Their Legal Rights and Moral Rights

Carl Wellman

Carl Wellman is the Lewin Distinguished Professor Emeritus in the Humanities at Washington University in Saint Louis and an honorary vice president of the International Association for the Philosophy of Law and Social Philosophy. In the following excerpt from his book Real Rights, *he discusses the question of how to resolve a conflict between legal rights and moral rights, using the case of* Gillette v. United States *as an example. Gillette was convicted of failure to report for induction into the armed services, claiming he was a conscientious objector (CO). He considered it his moral duty to refuse to fight in the Vietnam War, which he considered unjust, but because he was willing to fight in other wars he could not be classified as a CO. In court he argued that because he had a constitutional right to freedom of religion, his religious objection to unjust wars should be respected, but the Supreme Court ruled that his First Amendment rights*

Carl Wellman, *Real Rights*, Oxford University Press, 1995, pp. 234–38. Reproduced by permission of Oxford University Press.

had not been violated. Wellman concludes that someone thus torn between a legal duty and a moral duty must consider all the consequences and make a decision on the basis of practical reasoning.

How might one go about resolving a conflict between a legal right and a moral right? Legal reasoning would seem to leave the moral aspects of this conflict untouched, and moral reasoning has no relevance to the law except as it is recognized by some authoritative legal source. Thus, it is possible to reason about a conflict of rights only when one translates that conflict into some common denominator. Accordingly, there will typically be more than one resolution of any conflict between rights of entirely different species. In any given case, judicial reasoning might lead to one resolution and moral reasoning to quite a different resolution. What, then, is the moral agent caught in this practical predicament to do? The ultimate resolution will be by broadly practical reasoning, reasoning that takes into consideration every sort of practical reason—legal, moral, prudential, pragmatic, esthetic, and so on.

This sort of predicament is especially acute when some moral agent finds that a conflict of rights imposes on him two incompatible duties, one legal and the other moral. An illuminating example of this sort is provided by *Gillette v. United States.* Although the Supreme Court considered two appeals in this case, it will simplify our examination if we attend to only one of these, that of [Guy Porter] Gillette. [The Court stated:]

> Petitioner Gillette was convicted of willful failure to report for induction into the armed forces. Gillette defended on the ground that he should have been ruled exempt from induction as a conscientious objector to war. In support of his unsuccessful request for classification as a conscientious objector, this petitioner had stated his willingness to participate in a war of national defense or a war sponsored by the

United Nations as a peacekeeping measure, but declared his opposition to American military operations in Vietnam, which he characterized as "unjust."

From Gillette's viewpoint, he was morally required to refuse to perform his alleged legal duty to serve in the Vietnam War because of his moral duty not to participate in an unjust war. His legal duty was implied by the constitutional power-right of Congress to raise and support armies; his moral liberty to refuse to fulfill this duty was implied by Gillette's moral liberty-right to freedom of religion.

Legal Right to Religious Freedom

How did the Supreme Court of the United States resolve this conflict of rights? Gillette's moral right to religious freedom is legally relevant only insofar as it has been recognized in the law. The fundamental text is the very first part of the First Amendment that reads "Congress shall make no law respecting an establishment of religion, or prohibiting the free exercise thereof. . . ." Thus, the crucial issue before the court was whether a law that exempted from military service those who were conscientiously opposed to every war on religious grounds but denied such exemption to those who were conscientiously opposed to unjust wars only was unconstitutional because it violated this legal right.

Gillette had argued that Section 6(j) of the Military Selective Service Act of 1967 was inconsistent with the Establishment Clause because it gave a preferred status to members of those religious sects that advocated universal pacifism but disadvantaged those whose religious faith distinguished between the moral status of just and unjust wars. To this the Supreme Court replied:

> The critical weakness of petitioners' establishment claim arises from the fact that section 6(j), on its face, simply does not discriminate on the basis of religious affiliation or reli-

gious belief, apart of course from beliefs concerning war. The section says that anyone who is conscientiously opposed to all war shall be relieved of military service. The specified objection must have a grounding in "religious training and belief," but no particular sectarian affiliation or theological position is required.

Hence, it is not the purpose of this statute to establish any particular religion or religions and to discriminate against others.

Nevertheless, it could be argued that this section is unconstitutional because it results in de facto religious discrimination.

> Section 6(j) serves a number of valid purposes having nothing to do with a design to foster or favor any sect, religion, or cluster of religions. There are considerations of a pragmatic nature, such as the hopelessness of converting a sincere conscientious objector into an effective fighting man . . . , but no doubt the section reflects as well the view that "in the forum of conscience, duty to a moral power higher than the State has always been maintained."

But what important State purpose is served by excluding those who are conscientiously opposed only to unjust wars from exemption for military service?

Religious Neutrality of State Interests

> We conclude not only that the affirmative purposes underlying section 6(j) are neutral and secular, but also that valid neutral reasons exist for limiting the exemption to objectors to all war, and that the section therefore cannot be said to reflect a religious preference. Apart from the Government's need for manpower, perhaps the central interest involved in the administration of conscription laws is the interest in maintaining a fair system for determining "who serves when not all serve." . . . The contention is that the claim to relief on account of such objection is intrinsically a claim of un-

certain dimensions, and that granting that claim in theory would involve a real danger of erratic or even discriminatory decisionmaking in administrative practice.

Notice that here the judicial reasoning appeals to these important state interests, not as sufficient to override Gillette's constitutional right to freedom of religion, but to show by their neutrality that insofar as his right is defined by the Establishment Clause it is inapplicable to this case.

There remains, of course, Gillette's constitutional right to freedom of religion as defined by the Free Exercise Clause. After referring to the important state interests previously mentioned, the Supreme Court added:

However, the impact of conscription on objectors to particular wars is far from unjustified. The conscription laws, applied to such persons as to others, are not designed to interfere with any religious ritual or practice, and do not work a penalty against any theological position. The incidental burdens felt by persons in petitioners' position are strictly justified by substantial governmental interests that relate directly to the very impacts questioned. And more broadly, of course, there is the Government's interest in procuring the manpower necessary for military purposes, pursuant to the constitutional grant of power to Congress to raise and support armies.

In this passage, the Supreme Court advances two reasons why the contested section of the Military Selective Service Act of 1967 is not unconstitutional. First, it does not violate Gillette's constitutional right to freedom of religion as defined by the Free Exercise Clause, because the constraints it imposes on the right-holder are merely incidental and not directed against those practices of worship or theological beliefs at the heart of religion; second, this section of the Act is necessary to achieve state interests sufficient to override Gillette's right to the free exercise of his religious convictions. Because the former argument is not entirely persuasive, in the end, it is

the latter consideration that is decisive and that in the law re-
solves this conflict in favor of Congress's power-right to raise
and support armies and against Gillette's liberty-right to freedom of religion.

Moral Conflict Left Unresolved

Although this decision of the Supreme Court of the United
States is presumably definitive from the legal point of view, it
leaves the conflict between the legal right of Congress and
Gillette's moral right unresolved from the moral point of
view. Gillette still finds himself confronted with two incompatible duties—a legal duty to serve in the armed forces during the Vietnam War and a moral duty not to participate in
an unjust war. How might he resolve this dilemma by moral
reasoning?

He might well begin by appealing to a moral principle
recognized even by the court: "in the forum of conscience,
duty to a moral power higher than the State has always been
maintained." This principle functions in moral reasoning
much as the Supremacy Clause of the United States Constitution does in judicial reasoning to resolve conflicts between
laws issued by different authorities. Since God is a higher authority than man, one ought always to obey the law of God
even when so doing requires one to disobey the law of one's
society. Therefore, Gillette has the moral liberty of refusing to
obey the Selective Service Act because his moral right to religious freedom, endowed by his Creator, takes precedence over
the legal right of Congress to raise and support armies, con-
ferred by mere human lawmakers.

But can it be assumed without further argument that
Gillette's moral right to freedom of religion does confer on
him any liberty to disobey the law under the existing circumstances? After all, no right is unlimited and most admit of exceptions. Recall how the Court maintained that the Selective
Service Act imposed only incidental burdens on Gillette and

that refusing to exempt those who were conscientiously opposed only to particular wars was necessary to important state purposes. Whatever may be true from the legal point of view, from the moral point of view Gillette might well argue that being forced against his conscience to disobey the law of God and neglect his moral duty not to participate in an unjust war is hardly an incidental burden; it is to impose on him a mortal sin. He need not insist that the state is never morally justified in burdening the free exercise of one's religion. But he could, and probably should, distinguish between those laws that prohibit actions one's religion regards as virtuous or even saintly and laws that prevent or are intended to prevent one from fulfilling one's duties, actions strictly commanded by one's God and one's conscience. The former burdens may be justified by military or other necessity; the latter are never morally justified.

Although this moral reasoning is fairly straightforward and simple, it probably does not resolve this conflict of rights in a comfortable way. Why, from a specifically moral point of view, does the fact that Congress has a legal power-right to raise and support armies matter? It is because pursuant to that constitutional right Congress has enacted legislation that imposes a legal duty on Gillette and because Gillette does not deny that he has, at least under normal circumstances, a moral duty to obey the law of his state. Now his moral reasoning may well assure him that his obligation to obey the law is, in this particular case, overridden by his obligation to God and by his moral right to the free exercise of his religion. Still, he may believe, as many conscientious objectors do, that the state has a moral as well as a legal right to punish him for his disobedience and that he has a moral duty to submit to such punishment. To be sure, he need not take this additional step in his moral reasoning. Whether he does or not, he cannot, as a conscientious moral agent and a conscientious citizen, take this conflict between a moral right and a legal right lightly.

Resolving the Conflict

This recognition that Gillette is both a moral agent and a citizen of the United States reminds us that Gillette is now confronted with two resolutions of the conflict between his moral right to freedom of religion and the legal right of Congress to raise and support armies. The problem is that they reached conflicting conclusions. What is poor Gillette to do? He can hardly serve in the armed forces as a citizen and at the same time as a moral agent refuse to do so. If there is ultimately to be any overall resolution of this conflict of rights, it must be translated into some lowest common denominator. But what do judicial reasoning and moral reasoning have in common? In such cases, they are two species of practical reasoning. Thus, in the end, the final resolution must be by broadly practical reasoning—reasoning that takes into consideration every variety of reason for or against obeying the Selective Service Act.

How might Gillette, reasoning not merely as a moral agent but simply as an agent, resolve his dilemma? Let us begin with a consideration of the principle recognized in both the judicial and moral reasoning about this conflict of rights: "in the forum of conscience, duty to a moral power higher than the State has always been maintained." Does this principle hold true not merely in the forum of conscience but also in the forum of broadly practical reason? Well, why might the law of God be thought to be "higher" than the law of man? It could be because God is wiser and more benevolent than any mere human ruler or rulers so that His law is more certain to be beneficial. Or it might be because it would be imprudent to risk eternal damnation in order to avoid the temporary and less painful sanctions of one's legal system. Here prudential reasons become relevant and might reinforce the moral priority of religious duty over legal duty. Pragmatic and political reasons, such as the futility of America's war efforts in Vietnam or the probable impact of one's example on those parties working for the reform of our Government, might also bear on this conflict of rights. No doubt, to some, one's integrity and the difficulty of living with oneself if one were to violate one's conscience weighs heavily. In the end, each agent must consider a wide variety of practical reasons and resolve any such conflict between a legal right and a moral right by broadly practical reasoning.

 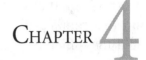

Trying Foreign Terrorists by Military Commission

Case Overview

Hamdan v. Rumsfeld (2006)

Salim Ahmed Hamdan, a citizen of Yemen, was being held at the American prison in Guantánamo Bay, Cuba. In 2001 he had been captured by militia forces and turned over to the U.S. military during the U.S. invasion of Afghanistan. He admitted to having been the personal driver and bodyguard for Al Qaeda leader Osama bin Laden. He was charged with conspiracy and providing material support for terrorism. President George W. Bush deemed him eligible to be tried (for then-unspecified offenses) by military commission, a form of trial historically used on battlefields for the quick dispatch of captured spies and other enemies. A year later, he was charged with conspiracy and providing material support for terrorism.

Although Hamdan conceded that a court-martial constituted in accordance with the Uniform Code of Military Justice would have authority to try him, he protested that the military commission the president had convened did not. Through his lawyers he filed a complaint saying neither any act of Congress nor the common law of war allowed trial by such a commission for the crime of conspiracy, which he said was not a violation of the law of war. Furthermore, Hamdan's lawyers claimed, the procedures that the president had adopted to try him would violate the most basic tenets of military and international law, including the principle that a defendant must be permitted to see and hear the evidence against him.

A district court ruled in favor of Hamdan, but the Court of Appeals reversed that decision. The Supreme Court agreed to review the case because "trial by military commission is an extraordinary measure raising important questions about the balance of powers in our constitutional structure." Although many government officials were named as defendants in the case, its title included only Donald Rumsfeld, who was then Secretary of Defense.

There was a great deal of public interest in the case because of the major controversy about what to do with al Qaeda terrorists who were captured outside the United States. They do not qualify as prisoners of war, since the war on terror is not a war between nations. They have not necessarily broken any U.S. laws, and yet they are clearly dangerous. At the time, there was no law specifying how they should be tried or what their rights were. Whether their treatment was covered under the international Geneva Conventions was hotly debated; the president said it was not, but many people believed that it was. There were many protests against conditions at the Guantánamo Bay prison, which the government said were not as bad as the critics claimed and were necessary for protecting the nation against terrorism. In addition, there was much political opposition to the policies of President Bush; his adversaries believed that he had assumed too much unilateral power, while his supporters held that he was entitled to it in his position as commander-in-chief of U.S. military forces.

The justices of the Supreme Court did not agree among themselves about the case. It was decided in Hamdan's favor by a five to three vote (the chief justice, John Roberts, did not participate because it was his own decision as a judge of the Court of Appeals that was being reviewed); however, one of the justices did not sign all sections of the exceptionally long opinion, so some of its sections had only plurality, rather than majority, support. Several justices wrote in a concurring opinion that although trial by military commissions was currently illegal, Congress could authorize it. There were also three separate dissenting opinions addressing various legal issues.

The outcome of the case was applauded by people who believed that foreign prisoners should have the same rights as American citizens, but it dismayed those concerned about the danger posed by terrorists. It also disturbed many who believed the Court had overstepped its bounds and should not be making war policy. To counteract the ruling and send a message to the Court to stay out of the war on terrorism, Congress soon passed the Military Commissions Act of 2006 (MCA), which authorized the use of military commissions to try noncitizens for war crimes. A year after the Supreme Court's decision, the charges against Hamdan were dropped on the grounds that the MCA applied only to "unlawful" enemy combatants, whereas he was classified merely as an enemy combatant. However, he was reclassified and charged again, found guilty, and given a prison sentence consisting mainly of time already served. Soon thereafter he was returned to Yemen, where in January 2009 he was released.

> "In undertaking to try [a foreign terror-
> ist] and subject him to criminal pun-
> ishment, the Executive is bound to
> comply with the Rule of Law that pre-
> vails in this jurisdiction."

Plurality Opinion: Foreign Terrorists Cannot Be Tried by U.S. Military Tribunals

John Paul Stevens

At the time of his retirement in 2010, John Paul Stevens was the oldest and longest-serving member of the Supreme Court and generally considered to be the leader of its liberal faction. In these excerpts from his extremely long and detailed opinion in Hamdan v. Rumsfeld, *he states that military commissions do not have authority to try cases of conspiracy and that Salim Hamdan was charged only with conspiracy, which he says is not a violation of the law of war. Even if it were, the planned military commission could not legally proceed, Stevens argues, because the law does not permit such commissions to have rules different from those of a court martial unless following court-martial rules would be impracticable, which the Court does believe has been proved. Furthermore, the Court believes the procedures to be used by the military commission would violate the Geneva Conventions, which require defendants other than prisoners in a war between nations to be tried by a regularly constituted court that provides all the judicial guarantees recognized as indispensable by civilized peoples.*

John Paul Stevens, plurality opinion, *Salim Ahmed Hamdan v. Donald H. Rumsfeld, Secretary of Defense, et al.*, U.S. Supreme Court, June 29, 2006. Reproduced by permission.

While we assume that the AUMF [Authorization for Use of Military Force] activated the President's war powers, and that those powers include the authority to convene military commissions in appropriate circumstances, there is nothing in the text or legislative history of the AUMF even hinting that Congress intended to expand or alter the authorization set forth in Article 21 of the UCMJ [Uniform Code of Military Justice].

Likewise, the DTA [Detainee Treatment Act] cannot be read to authorize this commission. Although the DTA, unlike either Article 21 or the AUMF, was enacted after the President had convened Hamdan's commission, it contains no language authorizing that tribunal or any other at Guantánamo Bay. . . .

Together, the UCMJ, the AUMF, and the DTA at most acknowledge a general Presidential authority to convene military commissions in circumstances where justified under the "Constitution and laws," including the law of war. Absent a more specific congressional authorization, the task of this Court is . . . to decide whether Hamdan's military commission is so justified. It is to that inquiry we now turn.

The common law governing military commissions may be gleaned from past practice and what sparse legal precedent exists. Commissions historically have been used in three situations. First, they have substituted for civilian courts at times and in places where martial law has been declared. . . . Second, commissions have been established to try civilians "as part of a temporary military government over occupied enemy territory or territory regained from an enemy where civilian government cannot and does not function." . . .

The third type of commission, convened as an "incident to the conduct of war" when there is a need "to seize and subject to disciplinary measures those enemies who in their attempt to thwart or impede our military effort have violated the law of war." . . . The last time the U. S. Armed Forces used the law-of-war military commission was during World War II. In

[*Ex parte*] *Quirin,* this Court sanctioned President [Franklin D.] Roosevelt's use of such a tribunal to try Nazi saboteurs captured on American soil during the War. And in *In Re Ya-mashita,* we held that a military commission had jurisdiction to try a Japanese commander for failing to prevent troops under his command from committing atrocities in the Philippines.

Quirin is the model the Government invokes most frequently to defend the commission convened to try Hamdan. That is both appropriate and unsurprising. Since Guantánamo Bay is neither enemy-occupied territory nor under martial law, the law-of-war commission is the only model available. At the same time, no more robust model of executive power exists; *Quirin* represents the high-water mark of military power to try enemy combatants for war crimes. . . .

A law-of-war commission has jurisdiction to try only two kinds of offense: "Violations of the laws and usages of war cognizable by military tribunals only," and "[b]reaches of military orders or regulations for which offenders are not legally triable by court-martial under the Articles of war." [Col. William Winthrope].

No Violation of Laws of War

The charge against Hamdan, alleges a conspiracy extending over a number of years, from 1996 to November 2001. All but two months of that more than 5-year-long period preceded the attacks of September 11, 2001, and the enactment of the AUMF—the Act of Congress on which the Government relies for exercise of its war powers and thus for its authority to convene military commissions. Neither the purported agreement with [Al Qaeda terrorist leader] Osama bin Laden and others to commit war crimes, nor a single overt act, is alleged to have occurred in a theater of war or on any specified date after September 11, 2001. None of the overt acts that Hamdan is alleged to have committed violates the law of war.

These facts alone cast doubt on the legality of the charge and, hence, the commission; as Winthrop makes plain, the offense alleged must have been committed both in a theater of war and *during*, not before, the relevant conflict. But the deficiencies in the time and place allegations also underscore—indeed are symptomatic of—the most serious defect of this charge: The offense it alleges is not triable by law-of-war military commission.

There is no suggestion that Congress has, in exercise of its constitutional authority to "define and punish ... Offences against the Law of Nations," positively identified "conspiracy" as a war crime. As we explained in *Quirin*, that is not necessarily fatal to the Government's claim of authority to try the alleged offense by military commission; Congress, through Article 21 of the UCMJ, has "incorporated by reference" the common law of war, which may render triable by military commission certain offenses not defined by statute. When, however, neither the elements of the offense nor the range of permissible punishments is defined by statute or treaty, the precedent must be plain and unambiguous. To demand any less would be to risk concentrating in military hands a degree of adjudicative and punitive power in excess of that contemplated either by statute or by the Constitution. . . .

At a minimum, the Government must make a substantial showing that the crime for which it seeks to try a defendant by military commission is acknowledged to be an offense against the law of war. That burden is far from satisfied here. The crime of "conspiracy" has rarely if ever been tried as such in this country by any law-of-war military commission not exercising some other form of jurisdiction, and does not appear in either the Geneva Conventions or the Hague Conventions—the major treaties on the law of war. . . .

If anything, *Quirin* supports Hamdan's argument that conspiracy is not a violation of the law of war. Not only did the Court pointedly omit any discussion of the conspiracy charge, but its analysis of Charge I placed special emphasis on the *completion* of an offense; it took seriously the saboteurs' argument that there can be no violation of a law of war—at least not one triable by military commission—without the actual commission of or attempt to commit a "hostile and warlike act."

That limitation makes eminent sense when one considers the necessity from whence this kind of military commission grew: The need to dispense swift justice, often in the form of execution, to illegal belligerents captured on the battlefield. The same urgency would not have been felt vis-à-vis enemies who had done little more than agree to violate the laws of war. . . .

Finally, international sources confirm that the crime charged here is not a recognized violation of the law of war. As observed above, none of the major treaties governing the law of war identifies conspiracy as a violation thereof. And the only "conspiracy" crimes that have been recognized by international war crimes tribunals (whose jurisdiction often extends beyond war crimes proper to crimes against humanity and crimes against the peace) are conspiracy to commit genocide and common plan to wage aggressive war, which is a crime against the peace and requires for its commission actual participation in a "concrete plan to wage war." . . .

Far from making the requisite substantial showing, the Government has failed even to offer a "merely colorable" case for inclusion of conspiracy among those offenses cognizable by law-of-war military commission. Because the charge does not support the commission's jurisdiction, the commission lacks authority to try Hamdan.

Trial by a Commission Unnecessary

The charge's shortcomings are not merely formal, but are indicative of a broader inability on the Executive's part here to satisfy the most basic precondition—at least in the absence of specific congressional authorization—for establishment of military commissions: military necessity. Hamdan's tribunal was appointed not by a military commander in the field of battle, but by a retired major general stationed away from any active hostilities. Hamdan is charged not with an overt act for which he was caught redhanded in a theater of war and which military efficiency demands be tried expeditiously, but with an *agreement* the inception of which long predated the attacks of September 11, 2001 and the AUMF. That may well be a crime, but it is not an offense that "by the law of war may be tried by military commissio[n]." None of the overt acts alleged to have been committed in furtherance of the agreement is itself a war crime, or even necessarily occurred during time of, or in a theater of, war. Any urgent need for imposition or execution of judgment is utterly belied by the record; Hamdan was arrested in November 2001 and he was not charged until mid-2004. These simply are not the circumstances in which, by any stretch of the historical evidence or this Court's precedents, a military commission established by Executive Order under the authority of Article 21 of the UCMJ may lawfully try a person and subject him to punishment.

Whether or not the Government has charged Hamdan with an offense against the law of war cognizable by military commission, the commission lacks power to proceed. The UCMJ conditions the President's use of military commissions on compliance not only with the American common law of war, but also with the rest of the UCMJ itself, insofar as applicable, and with the "rules and precepts of the law of nations." The procedures that the Government has decreed will govern Hamdan's trial by commission violate these laws. . . .

No Justification

The Government contends military commissions would be of no use if the President were hamstrung by those provisions of the UCMJ that govern courts-martial. Finally, the President's determination that "the danger to the safety of the United States and the nature of international terrorism" renders it impracticable "to apply in military commissions . . . the principles of law and rules of evidence generally recognized in the trial of criminal cases in the United States district courts," is, in the Government's view, explanation enough for any deviation from court-martial procedures.

Hamdan has the better of this argument. Without reaching the question whether any provision of Commission Order No. 1 is strictly "contrary to or inconsistent with" other provisions of the UCMJ, we conclude that the "practicability" determination the President has made is insufficient to justify variances from the procedures governing courts-martial. . . .

Assuming *arguendo* [for the sake of argument] that the reasons articulated in the President's Article 36(a) determination ought to be considered in evaluating the impracticability of applying court-martial rules, the only reason offered in support of that determination is the danger posed by international terrorism. Without for one moment underestimating that danger, it is not evident to us why it should require, in the case of Hamdan's trial, any variance from the rules that govern courts-martial.

The absence of any showing of impracticability is particularly disturbing when considered in light of the clear and admitted failure to apply one of the most fundamental protections afforded not just by the Manual for Courts-Martial but also by the UCMJ itself: the right to be present. Whether or not that departure technically is "contrary to or inconsistent with" the terms of the UCMJ, the jettisoning of so basic a right cannot lightly be excused as "practicable." . . .

Under the circumstances, then, the rules applicable in courts-martial must apply. Since it is undisputed that Commission Order No. 1 deviates in many significant respects from those rules, it necessarily violates Article 36(b). . . .

That Article not having been complied with here, the rules specified for Hamdan's trial are illegal.

Violation of the Geneva Conventions

The procedures adopted to try Hamdan also violate the Geneva Conventions. The Court of Appeals dismissed Hamdan's Geneva Convention challenge on three independent grounds: (1) the Geneva Conventions are not judicially enforceable; (2) Hamdan in any event is not entitled to their protections; and (3) even if he is entitled to their protections, [*Schlesinger v.*] *Councilman* abstention is appropriate.... The abstention rule applied in *Councilman*, is not applicable here. And for the reasons that follow, we hold that neither of the other grounds the Court of Appeals gave for its decision is persuasive....

The conflict with al Qaeda is not, according to the Government, a conflict to which the full protections afforded detainees under the 1949 Geneva Conventions apply because Article 2 of those Conventions (which appears in all four Conventions) renders the full protections applicable only to "all cases of declared war or of any other armed conflict which may arise between two or more of the High Contracting Parties." Since Hamdan was captured and detained incident to the conflict with al Qaeda and not the conflict with the Taliban, and since al Qaeda, unlike Afghanistan, is not a "High Contracting Party"—*i.e.*, a signatory of the Conventions, the protections of those Conventions are not, it is argued, applicable to Hamdan.

We need not decide the merits of this argument because there is at least one provision of the Geneva Conventions that applies here even if the relevant conflict is not one between signatories. Article 3, often referred to as Common Article 3 because, like Article 2, it appears in all four Geneva Conventions, provides that in a "conflict not of an international character occurring in the territory of one of the High Contracting Parties, each Party to the conflict shall be bound to apply, as a minimum," certain provisions protecting "[p]ersons taking no active part in the hostilities, including members of armed forces who have laid down their arms and those placed *hors de combat* [incapable of fighting] by . . . detention." One such provision prohibits "the passing of sentences and the carrying out of executions without previous judgment pronounced by a regularly constituted court affording all the judicial guarantees which are recognized as indispensable by civilized peoples."

The Court of Appeals thought, and the Government asserts, that Common Article 3 does not apply to Hamdan because the conflict with al Qaeda, being "'international in scope,'" does not qualify as a "'conflict not of an international character.'" That reasoning is erroneous. The term "conflict not of an international character" is used here in contradistinction to a conflict between nations. . . . Common Article 3, . . . affords some minimal protection, falling short of full protection under the Conventions, to individuals associated with neither a signatory nor even a nonsignatory "Power" who are involved in a conflict "in the territory of" a signatory. The latter kind of conflict is distinguishable from the conflict described in Common Article 2 chiefly because it does not involve a clash between nations (whether signatories or not). In context, then, the phrase "not of an international character" bears its literal meaning.

Although the official commentaries accompanying Common Article 3 indicate that an important purpose of the provision was to furnish minimal protection to rebels involved in one kind of "conflict not of an international character," *i.e.*, a civil war, the commentaries also make clear "that the scope of the Article must be as wide as possible." . . .

Regular Judicial Guarantees Needed

Common Article 3, then, is applicable here and, as indicated above, requires that Hamdan be tried by a "regularly constituted court affording all the judicial guarantees which are recognized as indispensable by civilized peoples." . . . One of the Red Cross' own treatises defines "regularly constituted court" as used in Common Article 3 to mean "established and organized in accordance with the laws and procedures already in force in a country."

The Government offers only a cursory defense of Hamdan's military commission in light of Common Article 3. . . .

Inextricably intertwined with the question of regular constitution is the evaluation of the procedures governing the tribunal and whether they afford "all the judicial guarantees which are recognized as indispensable by civilized peoples." Like the phrase "regularly constituted court," this phrase is not defined in the text of the Geneva Conventions. But it must be understood to incorporate at least the barest of those trial protections that have been recognized by customary international law. . . .

Various provisions of Commission Order No. 1 dispense with the principles, articulated in Article 75 and indisputably part of the customary international law, that an accused must, absent disruptive conduct or consent, be present for his trial and must be privy to the evidence against him. That the Government has a compelling interest in denying Hamdan access to certain sensitive information is not doubted. But, at least absent express statutory provision to the contrary, information used to convict a person of a crime must be disclosed to him. . . .

We have assumed, as we must, that the allegations made in the Government's charge against Hamdan are true. We have assumed, moreover, the truth of the message implicit in that charge—viz., that Hamdan is a dangerous individual whose beliefs, if acted upon, would cause great harm and even death to innocent civilians, and who would act upon those beliefs if given the opportunity. It bears emphasizing that Hamdan does not challenge, and we do not today address, the

Government's power to detain him for the duration of active hostilities in order to prevent such harm. But in undertaking to try Hamdan and subject him to criminal punishment, the Executive is bound to comply with the Rule of Law that prevails in this jurisdiction.

> "The [Court's] willingness to second-
> guess the Executive's judgments . . .
> constitutes an unprecedented departure
> from the traditionally limited role of
> the courts with respect to war."

Dissenting Opinion: The Court Should Not Override the President's Authority to Determine How Foreign Terrorists Will Be Tried

Clarence Thomas

Clarence Thomas, the second African American to serve on the Supreme Court, has been a justice since 1991. He is among the Court's most conservative members. In the following excerpts from his long dissenting opinion in Hamdan v. Rumsfeld, *he argues that the Court's overruling of the president's decisions in the war against terrorism is contrary to all past precedents concerning war issues. Moreover, he says, the Court's contention that Hamdan was charged only with conspiracy and not with overt acts is not true; although contrary to the majority's ruling, conspiracy to massacre innocent civilians alone does violate the laws of war. In Thomas's opinion, by ruling that the planned trial by a military commission violates the Geneva Conventions, the Court has ignored the provisions of those conventions with which*

Clarence Thomas, dissenting opinion, *Salim Ahmed Hamdan v. Donald H. Rumsfeld, Secretary Of Defense. et al.*, U.S. Supreme Court, June 29, 2006. Reproduced by permission.

it disagrees. He maintains that military commissions can conduct fair trials and that the President's authority as commander-in-chief should be respected.

The plurality concludes that the legality of the charge against [Salim Ahmed] Hamdan is doubtful because "Hamdan is charged not with an overt act for which he was caught redhanded in a theater of war . . . but with an *agreement* the inception of which long predated . . . the [relevant armed conflict]." (emphasis in original). The plurality's willingness to second-guess the Executive's judgments in this context, based upon little more than its unsupported assertions, constitutes an unprecedented departure from the traditionally limited role of the courts with respect to war and an unwarranted intrusion on executive authority. And even if such second-guessing were appropriate, the plurality's attempt to do so is unpersuasive.

As an initial matter, the plurality relies upon the date of the AUMF's [Authorization for the Use of Military Force] enactment to determine the beginning point for the "period of the war," thereby suggesting that petitioner's commission does not have jurisdiction to try him for offenses committed prior to the AUMF's enactment. But this suggestion betrays the plurality's unfamiliarity with the realities of warfare and its willful blindness to our precedents. The starting point of the present conflict (or indeed any conflict) is not determined by congressional enactment, but rather by the initiation of hostilities. . . .

The President's judgment—that the present conflict substantially predates the AUMF, extending at least as far back as al Qaeda's 1996 declaration of war on our Nation, and that the theater of war extends at least as far as the localities of al Qaeda's principal bases of operations—is beyond judicial reproach. And the plurality's unsupportable contrary determination merely confirms that "'the Judiciary has neither aptitude, facilities nor responsibility'" [*Chicago & Southern Air Lines v. Waterman S.S. Corp.* (1948)] for making military or foreign affairs judgments. . . .

The Common Law of War

Law-of-war military commissions have jurisdiction over "'individuals of the enemy's army who have been guilty of illegitimate warfare or other offences in violation of the laws of war,'" (quoting [Col. William] Winthrop). They also have jurisdiction over "[i]rregular armed bodies or persons not forming part of the organized forces of a belligerent" "who would not be likely to respect the laws of war." . . . This consideration is easily satisfied here, as Hamdan is an unlawful combatant charged with joining and conspiring with a terrorist network dedicated to flouting the laws of war. . . .

Whether an offense is a violation of the law of war cognizable before a military commission must be determined pursuant to "the system of common law applied by military tribunals." *Ex parte Quirin.*

The common law of war as it pertains to offenses triable by military commission is derived from the "experience of our wars" and our wartime tribunals, and "the laws and usages of war as understood and practiced by the civilized nations of the world." Opinion of the Attorney General. Moreover, the common law of war is marked by two important features. First, as with the common law generally, it is flexible and evolutionary in nature, building upon the experience of the past and taking account of the exigencies of the present. . . . Second, the common law of war affords a measure of respect for the judgment of military commanders. Thus, "[t]he commander of an army in time of war has the same power to organize military tribunals and execute their judgments that he has to set his squadrons in the field and fight battles. His authority in each case is from the law and usage of war." In recognition of these principles, Congress has generally "'left it to the President, and the military commanders representing him, to employ the commission, *as occasion may require*, for the investigation and punishment of violations of the law of war.'" (Winthrop; emphasis added).

In one key respect, the plurality departs from the proper framework for evaluating the adequacy of the charge against Hamdan under the laws of war. The plurality holds that where, as here, "neither the elements of the offense nor the range of permissible punishments is defined by statute or treaty, the precedent [establishing whether an offense is triable by military commission] must be plain and unambiguous." This is a pure contrivance, and a bad one at that. It is contrary to the presumption we acknowledged in *Quirin*, namely, that the actions of military commissions are "not to be set aside by the courts without the *clear conviction* that they are" unlawful, (emphasis added). . . .

The plurality's newly minted clear-statement rule is also fundamentally inconsistent with the nature of the common law which, by definition, evolves and develops over time . . . Though the charge against Hamdan easily satisfies even the plurality's manufactured rule, the plurality's inflexible approach has dangerous implications for the Executive's ability to discharge his duties as Commander in Chief in future cases. We should undertake to determine whether an unlawful combatant has been charged with an offense against the law of war with an understanding that the common law of war is flexible, responsive to the exigencies of the present conflict, and deferential to the judgment of military commanders. . . .

The Charges Against Hamdan

The common law of war establishes that Hamdan's willful and knowing membership in al Qaeda is a war crime chargeable before a military commission. Hamdan, a confirmed enemy combatant and member or affiliate of al Qaeda, has been charged with willfully and knowingly joining a group (al

Qaeda) whose purpose is "to support violent attacks against property and nationals (both military and civilian) of the United States." Moreover, the allegations specify that Hamdan joined and maintained his relationship with al Qaeda even though he "believed that [al Qaeda leader] Osama bin Laden and his associates were involved in the attacks on the U.S. Embassies in Kenya and Tanzania in August 1998, the attack on the USS COLE in October 2000, and the attacks on the United States on September 11, 2001." These allegations, against a confirmed unlawful combatant, are alone sufficient to sustain the jurisdiction of Hamdan's military commission.

For well over a century it has been established that "to unite with banditti, jayhawkers, guerillas, or any other unauthorized marauders is a high offence against the laws of war; *the offence is complete when the band is organized or joined. The atrocities committed by such a band do not constitute the offence, but make the reasons, and sufficient reasons they are, why such banditti are denounced by the laws of war.*" 11 Op. Atty. Gen., (emphasis added). . . .

Moreover, the Government has alleged that Hamdan was not only a member of al Qaeda while it was carrying out terrorist attacks on civilian targets in the United States and abroad, but also that Hamdan aided and assisted al Qaeda's top leadership by supplying weapons, transportation, and other services. These allegations further confirm that Hamdan is triable before a law-of-war military commission for his involvement with al Qaeda. . . .

Separate and apart from the offense of joining a contingent of "uncivilized combatants who [are] not . . . likely to respect the laws of war," Winthrop 784, Hamdan has been charged with "conspir[ing] and agree[ing] with . . . the al Qaida organization . . . to commit . . . offenses triable by military commission". Those offenses include "attacking civilians; attacking civilian objects; murder by an unprivileged belligerent; and terrorism." This, too, alleges a violation of the law of war triable by military commission. . . .

Winthrop says nothing to exclude either conspiracy or membership in a criminal enterprise, both of which go beyond "intentions merely" and "consis[t] of *overt acts, i.e.* . . . unlawful commissions or actual attempts to commit," and both of which are *expressly* recognized by Winthrop as crimes against the law of war triable by military commissions. Indeed, the commission of an *"overt ac[t]"* is the traditional requirement for the completion of the crime of conspiracy, and the charge against Hamdan alleges numerous such overt acts. . . . Hamdan has been charged with the overt acts of providing protection, transportation, weapons, and other services to the enemy, acts which in and of themselves are violations of the laws of war. . . .

Terrorists Must Be Held Accountable

Today a plurality of this Court would hold that conspiracy to massacre innocent civilians does not violate the laws of war. This determination is unsustainable. The judgment of the political branches that Hamdan, and others like him, must be held accountable before military commissions for their involvement with and membership in an unlawful organization dedicated to inflicting massive civilian casualties is supported by virtually every relevant authority, including all of the authorities invoked by the plurality today. It is also supported by the nature of the present conflict. We are not engaged in a traditional battle with a nation-state, but with a worldwide, hydraheaded enemy, who lurks in the shadows conspiring to reproduce the atrocities of September 11, 2001, and who has boasted of sending suicide bombers into civilian gatherings, has proudly distributed videotapes of beheadings of civilian workers, and has tortured and dismembered captured American soldiers. But according to the plurality, when our Armed Forces capture those who are plotting terrorist atrocities like the bombing of the Khobar Towers [in Saudi Arabia], the bombing of the U.S.S. *Cole*, and the attacks of September 11—even if their plots are advanced to the very brink of fulfillment—our military cannot charge those criminals with any offense against the laws of war. Instead, our troops must catch the terrorists "redhanded," in the midst of *the attack itself*, in order to bring them to justice. Not only is this conclusion fundamentally inconsistent with the cardinal principal of the law of war, namely protecting non-combatants, but it would sorely hamper the President's ability to confront and defeat a new and deadly enemy. . . .

The Court's conclusion that Article 36(b) requires the President to apply the same rules and procedures to military commissions as are applicable to courts-martial is unsustainable. When Congress codified Article 15 of the Articles of War in Article 21 of the UCMJ [Uniform Code of Military Justice] it was "presumed to be aware of . . . and to adopt" this Court's interpretation of that provision as preserving the common-law status of military commissions, inclusive of the President's unfettered authority to prescribe their procedures. *Lorillard v. Pons.* . . .

Nothing in the text of Article 36(b) supports the Court's sweeping conclusion that it represents an unprecedented congressional effort to change the nature of military commissions from common-law war courts to tribunals that must presumptively function like courts-martial. And such an interpretation would be strange indeed. The vision of uniformity that motivated the adoption of the UCMJ, embodied specifically in Article 36(b), is nothing more than uniformity across the separate branches of the armed services. There is no indication that the UCMJ was intended to require uniformity in procedure between courts-martial and military commissions, tribunals that the UCMJ itself recognizes are different. . . . Consistent with this Court's prior interpretations of Article 21 and over a century of historical practice, it cannot be understood to require the President to conform the procedures employed by military commissions to those employed by courts-martial.

Even if Article 36(b) could be construed to require procedural uniformity among the various tribunals contemplated by the UCMJ, Hamdan would not be entitled to relief. Under the Court's reading, the President is entitled to prescribe different rules for military commissions than for courts-martial when he determines that it is not "practicable" to prescribe uniform rules. The Court does not resolve the level of deference such determinations would be owed, however, because, in its view, "[t]he President has not . . . [determined] that it is impracticable to apply the rules for courts-martial." This is simply not the case. . . . The President reached this conclusion because

> we're in the middle of a war, and . . . had to design a procedure that would allow us to pursue justice for these individuals while at the same time prosecuting the war most effectively. And that means setting rules that would allow us to preserve our intelligence secrets, develop more information about terrorist activities that might be planned for the future so that we can take action to prevent terrorist attacks against the United States. . . . [T]here was a constant balancing of the requirements of our war policy and the importance of providing justice for individuals . . . and *each* deviation from the standard kinds of rules that we have in our criminal courts was motivated by the desire to strike the balance between individual justice and the broader war policy. *Ibid.* (remarks of Douglas J. Feith, Under Secretary of Defense for Policy (emphasis added)). . . .

The plurality further contends that Hamdan's commission is unlawful because it fails to provide him the right to be present at his trial. . . . But [the law cited] applies to courts-martial, not military commissions. . . .

Geneva Conventions Not Applicable

The Court contends that Hamdan's military commission is also unlawful because it violates Common Article 3 of the Geneva Conventions. Furthermore, Hamdan contends that his commission is unlawful because it violates various provisions of the Third Geneva Convention. These contentions are untenable.

As an initial matter, and as the Court of Appeals concluded, both of Hamdan's Geneva Convention claims are foreclosed by *Johnson v. Eisentrager*. In that case the respondents claimed, *inter alia* [among other things], that their military commission lacked jurisdiction because it failed to provide them with certain procedural safeguards that they argued were required under the Geneva Conventions. While this Court rejected the underlying merits of the respondents' Geneva Convention claims, it also held, in the alternative, that the respondents could "not assert . . . that anything in the Geneva Convention makes them immune from prosecution or punishment for war crimes." . . .

The provisions of the 1929 Geneva Convention were not judicially enforceable because that Convention contemplated that diplomatic measures by political and military authorities were the exclusive mechanisms for such enforcement. . . .

The Court's position thus rests on the assumption that Article 21's reference to the "laws of war" selectively incorporates only those aspects of the Geneva Conventions that the Court finds convenient, namely, the substantive requirements of Common Article 3, and not those aspects of the Conventions that the Court, for whatever reason, disfavors, namely the Conventions' exclusive diplomatic enforcement scheme. The Court provides no account of why the *partial* incorporation of the Geneva Conventions should extend only so far—and no further—because none is available beyond its evident preference to adjudicate those matters that the law of war, through the Geneva Conventions, consigns exclusively to the political branches.

Even if the Court were correct that Article 21 of the UCMJ renders judicially enforceable aspects of the law of war that are not so enforceable by their own terms, Article 21 simply cannot be interpreted to render judicially enforceable the particular provision of the law of war at issue here, namely Common Article 3 of the Geneva Conventions. As relevant, Article 21 provides that "[t]he provisions of this chapter conferring jurisdiction upon courts-martial do not deprive military commissions . . . of concurrent jurisdiction with respect to *offenders or offenses* that by statute *or by the law of war* may be tried by military commissions." (emphasis added). . . .

In addition to being foreclosed by *Eisentrager*, Hamdan's claim under Common Article 3 of the Geneva Conventions is meritless. Common Article 3 applies to "armed conflict not of an international character occurring in the territory of one of the High Contracting Parties." . . .

The conflict with al Qaeda is international in character in the sense that it is occurring in various nations around the globe. Thus, it is also "occurring in the territory of" more than "one of the High Contracting Parties." The Court does not dispute the President's judgments respecting the nature of our conflict with al Qaeda, nor does it suggest that the President's interpretation of Common Article 3 is implausible or foreclosed by the text of the treaty. Indeed, the Court concedes that Common Article 3 is principally concerned with "furnish[ing] minimal protection to rebels involved in . . . a civil war," precisely the type of conflict the President's interpretation envisions to be subject to Common Article 3. Instead, the Court, without acknowledging its duty to defer to the President, adopts its own, admittedly plausible, reading of Common Article 3. But where, as here, an ambiguous treaty provision ("not of an international character") is susceptible of two plausible, and reasonable, interpretations, our precedents require us to defer to the Executive's interpretation.

Trial Procedures Not Prohibited

But even if Common Article 3 were judicially enforceable and applicable to the present conflict, petitioner would not be entitled to relief. As an initial matter, any claim petitioner has under Common Article 3 is not ripe. The only relevant "acts" that "are and shall remain prohibited" under Common Article 3 are "the *passing of sentences* and the *carrying out of executions* without previous judgment pronounced by a regularly constituted court affording all the judicial guarantees which are recognized as indispensable by civilized peoples." (emphases added). As its terms make clear, Common Article 3 is only violated, as relevant here, by the act of "passing of sentenc[e]," and thus Hamdan will only have a claim *if* his military commission convicts him and imposes a sentence. . . . Indeed, even if we assume he will be convicted and sentenced, whether his trial will be conducted in a manner so as to deprive him of "the judicial guarantees which are recognized as indispensable by civilized peoples" is entirely speculative. . . .

In any event, Hamdan's military commission complies with the requirements of Common Article 3. It is plainly "regularly constituted" because such commissions have been employed throughout our history to try unlawful combatants for crimes against the law of war. . . .

Hamdan's commission has been constituted in accordance with these historical precedents. As I have previously explained, the procedures to be employed by that commission, and the Executive's authority to alter those procedures, are consistent with the practice of previous American military commissions. . . .

The procedures to be employed by Hamdan's commission afford "all the judicial guarantees which are recognized as indispensable by civilized peoples." . . .

The plurality concludes that Hamdan's commission is unlawful because of the possibility that Hamdan will be barred from proceedings and denied access to evidence that may be used to convict him. But, under the commissions' rules, the Government may not impose such bar or denial on Hamdan if it would render his trial unfair, a question that is clearly within the scope of the appellate review contemplated by regulation and statute.

Moreover, while the Executive is surely not required to offer a particularized defense of these procedures prior to their application, the procedures themselves make clear that Hamdan would only be excluded (other than for disruption) if it were necessary to protect classified (or classifiable) intelligence, including the sources and methods for gathering such intelligence. . . . According to the Government, "[b]ecause al Qaeda operates as a clandestine force relying on sleeper agents to mount surprise attacks, one of the most critical fronts in the current war involves gathering intelligence about future terrorist attacks and how the terrorist network operates— identifying where its operatives are, how it plans attacks, who directs operations, and how they communicate." We should not rule out the possibility that this compelling interest can be protected, while at the same time affording Hamdan (and others like him) a fair trial.

In these circumstances, "civilized peoples" would take into account the context of military commission trials against unlawful combatants in the war on terrorism, including the need to keep certain information secret in the interest of preventing future attacks on our Nation and its foreign installations so long as it did not deprive the accused of a fair trial. Accordingly, the President's understanding of the requirements of Common Article 3 is entitled to "great weight."

In addition to Common Article 3, which applies to conflicts "not of an international character," Hamdan also claims that he is entitled to the protections of the Third Geneva

Convention, which applies to conflicts between two or more High Contracting Parties. There is no merit to Hamdan's claim.

Article 2 of the Convention provides that "the present Convention shall apply to all cases of declared war or of any other armed conflict which may arise between two or more of the High Contracting Parties." "Pursuant to [his] authority as Commander in Chief and Chief Executive of the United States," the President has determined that the Convention is inapplicable here, explaining that "none of the provisions of Geneva apply to our conflict with al Qaeda in Afghanistan or elsewhere throughout the world, because, among other reasons, al Qaeda is not a High Contracting Party." The President's findings about the nature of the present conflict with respect to members of al Qaeda operating in Afghanistan represents a core exercise of his commander-in-chief authority that this Court is bound to respect.

> "[The Court's ruling] is a grotesque and
> unfixable misreading of the Geneva
> Conventions."

The Court Misinterpreted
International Treaties on the
Treatment of War Prisoners

Charles Krauthammer

*Charles Krauthammer is a Pulitzer Prize–winning syndicated
columnist and a regular panelist on television's Fox News. In the
following column he expresses dismay at the Supreme Court's
decision in* Hamdan v. Rumsfeld, *saying that the Court in effect
declared that the national emergency created by the attack of
September 11, 2001, is over, when in fact the war on terrorism
continues. It was a bad ruling, he says, because it disregarded
the intent of Congress with regard to the president's establishment of military tribunals, and worse, it misinterpreted the
Geneva Conventions. The first problem can be fixed by Congress
through a new law, but the second cannot, and in Krauthammer's
opinion it gives terrorists legal protections that were not intended
for unlawful combatants.*

1 861. 1941. 2001. Our big wars—and the war on terrorism
ranks with the big ones—have a way of starting in the first
year of a decade. Supreme Courts, which historically have
been loath to intervene against presidential war powers in the
midst of conflict, have tended to give the president until mid-
decade to do what he wishes to the Constitution in order to
win the war.

Charles Krauthammer, "Emergency over, Saith the Court," *Washington Post*, July 7, 2006.
Copyright © 2006 The Washington Post Company. Reproduced by permission of the
author.

During the Civil War, Abraham Lincoln suspended the writ of habeas corpus [the right to be brought to court rather than held without a specific charge]—trashing the Bill of Rights or exercising necessary emergency executive power, depending on your point of view. But he got the whole troublesome business done by 1865, and the Supreme Court stayed away.

During World War II, Franklin Roosevelt interned Japanese Americans. He, too, was left unmolested by the court. But Roosevelt also got his war wrapped up by 1945. Had the current war on terrorism followed course and ended in 2005, the sensational, just-decided [in 2006] *Hamdan v. Rumsfeld* case concerning military tribunals for Guantanamo Bay prisoners would have either been rendered moot or drawn a yawn.

But, of course, the war on terrorism is different. The enemy is shadowy, scattered and therefore more likely to survive and keep the war going for years. What the Supreme Court essentially did in *Hamdan* was to say to the president: Time's up. We gave you the customary half-decade of emergency powers, but that's as far as we go. From now on the emergency is over, at least judicially, and you're going to have to operate by peacetime rules.

Or, as Justice Anthony Kennedy, the new Sandra Day O'Connor, put it, Guantanamo (and by extension, war-on-terrorism) jurisprudence must henceforth be governed by "the customary operation of the Executive and Legislative Branches." This case may be "of extraordinary importance," but it is to be "resolved by ordinary rules."

All rise: The Supreme Court has decreed a return to normality. A lovely idea, except that al-Qaeda has other ideas. The war does go on. One can sympathize with the court's desire for a [president Warren G.] Harding-like restoration to normalcy. But the robed eminences are premature. And even if they weren't, they really didn't have to issue a ruling this bad.

A Bad Ruling

They declared illegal President [George W.] Bush's military tribunals for the likes of Salim Ahmed Hamdan, Osama bin Laden's driver and bodyguard. First, because they were not established in accordance with congressional authority. And, second, because they violated the Geneva Conventions.

The first rationale is an odd but fixable misreading of congressional intent. The second is a grotesque and unfixable misreading of the Geneva Conventions.

The court feels that the president slighted Congress by unilaterally establishing military commissions. What is odd about this solicitousness for the powers of the legislature is that Congress, which is populated entirely by adults, had explicitly told the judiciary just six months ago that when it comes to Guantanamo prisoners, the judiciary should bug off.

The Detainee Treatment Act in December 2005 not only implicitly endorsed what the administration was doing with prisoners, it explicitly told the judiciary to leave the issue to Congress and the president to resolve, as they have historically.

The court's wanton overriding of Congress and the president is another in a long string of breathtaking acts of judicial arrogance. But it is fixable. The Republican leadership of the Senate responded to the court's highhandedness by immediately embarking on writing legislation to establish military tribunals.

The unfixable part of the *Hamdan* ruling, however, is the court's reading of Common Article 3 of the Geneva Conventions. The Geneva Conventions, which were designed to protect civilian populations and those combatants who respect them, were never intended to apply to unlawful combatants, terrorists of the al-Qaeda kind. The court tortures the reading of Common Article 3 to confer upon Hamdan—and by extension the man for whom he rode shotgun, bin Laden—the kind of elaborate legal protections that one expects from "civilized peoples."

This infinitely elastic concept will allow courts to usurp from Congress and the president the authority to fashion the procedures for military tribunals—an arrogation that mocks the court's previously expressed solicitousness for congressional authority.

But no matter. Logic has little place here. The court has decreed: There is no war—or we will pretend so—and henceforth it shall be conducted by the court. God save the United States. (This honorable court can fend for itself.)

| "The [George W. Bush] administration has ... sought to evade the limitations set by international law on coercive interrogation ... of its detainees."

The President's Treatment of Imprisoned Terrorists Violated International Law

David Cole

David Cole is a professor at Georgetown University Law Center. In the following viewpoint he praises the Supreme Court's decision in Hamdan v. Rumsfeld, *saying that it was a good thing for the Court to stand up to the president, who, in his opinion, had established policies that violate human rights. Cole says that the ruling that it was against the law to set up military tribunals to try enemy combatants, and that these tribunals violated the Geneva Conventions, has implications for other controversial issues in the war on terror, such as the methods used for interrogating prisoners. He argues that some of the actions of the George W. Bush administration are war crimes under international law, and that it is important for the United States to conform to international law.*

Since the first few days after the terrorist attacks of September 11, 2001, the [George W.] Bush administration has taken the view that the President has unilateral, unchecked authority to wage a war, not only against those who attacked us on that day, but against all terrorist organizations of poten-

David Cole, "Why the Court Said No," *New York Review of Books*, August 10, 2006. Copyright © 2006 by NYREV, Inc. Reprinted with permission from The New York Review of Books.

tially global reach. The administration claims that the President's role as commander in chief of the armed forces grants him exclusive authority to select "the means and methods of engaging the enemy." And it has interpreted that power in turn to permit the President to take actions many consider illegal. . . .

He has asserted the right to imprison indefinitely, without hearings, anyone he considers an "enemy combatant," and to try such persons for war crimes in ad hoc military tribunals lacking such essential safeguards as independent judges and the right of the accused to confront the evidence against him.

In advocating these positions, which I will collectively call "the Bush doctrine," the administration has brushed aside legal objections as mere hindrances to the ultimate goal of keeping Americans safe. It has argued that domestic criminal and constitutional law are of little concern because the President's powers as commander in chief override all such laws; that the Geneva Conventions, a set of international treaties that regulate the treatment of prisoners during war, simply do not apply to the conflict with al-Qaeda; and more broadly still, that the President has unilateral authority to defy international law. . . .

If another nation's leader adopted such positions, the United States would be quick to condemn him or her for violating fundamental tenets of the rule of law, human rights, and the separation of powers. But President Bush has largely gotten away with it, at least at home. . . .

These realities make the Supreme Court's decision in *Hamdan v. Rumsfeld*, issued on the last day of its 2005–2006 term, in equal parts stunning and crucial. Stunning because the Court, unlike Congress, the opposition party, or the American people, actually stood up to the President. Crucial because the Court's decision, while on the surface narrowly focused on whether the military tribunals President Bush created to try foreign suspects for war crimes were consistent with US law, marked, at a deeper level, a dramatic refutation of the administration's entire approach to the "war on terror."

At bottom, the *Hamdan* case stands for the proposition that the rule of law—including international law—is not subservient to the will of the executive, even during wartime. As Justice John Paul Stevens wrote in the concluding lines of his opinion for the majority:

> In undertaking to try Hamdan and subject him to criminal punishment, the Executive is bound to comply with the Rule of Law that prevails in this jurisdiction.

The notion that government must abide by law is hardly radical. Its implications for the "war on terror" are radical, however, precisely because the Bush doctrine has so fundamentally challenged that very idea.

Military Tribunals

Salim Hamdan, a citizen of Yemen, has been held at Guantánamo Bay since June 2002. He is one of only fourteen men at Guantánamo who have been designated by the administration to be tried for war crimes—the remaining 440 or so have never been charged with any criminal conduct. Hamdan was charged with conspiracy to commit war crimes by serving as Osama bin Laden's driver and bodyguard, and by attending an al-Qaeda training camp.

The tribunal set up to try Hamdan was created by an executive order issued in November 2001. Its rules are draconian. They permit defendants to be tried and convicted on the basis of evidence that neither they nor their chosen civilian lawyers have any chance to see or rebut. They allow the use of hearsay evidence, which similarly deprives the defendant of an opportunity to cross-examine his accuser. They exclude information obtained by torture, but permit testimony coerced by any means short of torture. They deny the defendant the right to be present at all phases of his own trial. They empower the secretary of defense or his subordinate to intervene in the trial and decide central issues in the case instead of the presiding judge. And finally, the rules are predicated on a double standard, since these procedures apply only to foreign nationals accused of acts of terrorism, not US citizens.

Hamdan's lawyers challenged the legality of the military tribunals in federal court before his trial had even begun, arguing that the President lacked authority to create the tribunals in the first place, and that the tribunals' structure and procedures violated the Constitution, US military law, and the Geneva Conventions.

To say that Hamdan faced an uphill battle is a gross understatement. The Supreme Court has said in the past that foreign nationals who are outside US borders, like Hamdan, lack any constitutional protections. Hamdan was a member of the enemy forces when he was captured, and courts are especially reluctant to interfere with the military's treatment of "enemy aliens" in wartime. He filed his suit before trial, and courts generally prefer to wait until a trial is completed before assessing its legality. And as recently as World War II, the Supreme Court upheld the use of military tribunals, and ruled that the Geneva Conventions are not enforceable by individuals in US courts but may be enforced only through diplomatic means.

Surprisingly, Hamdan prevailed in the district court, when US District Judge James Robertson courageously ruled that trying Hamdan in a military tribunal of the kind set up by the government would violate the Geneva Conventions. Not surprisingly, that decision was unanimously reversed, on every conceivable ground, by the Court of Appeals for the D.C. Circuit, in an opinion joined fully by then Judge, now Chief Justice, John Roberts. And as if Hamdan did not face enough hurdles, after the Supreme Court agreed to hear his case, Congress passed a law that appeared to be designed to strip the Supreme Court of its jurisdiction to hear the case. The Detainee Treatment Act of 2005 required defendants in military tribunals to undergo their trials before seeking judicial review, and prescribed the D.C. Circuit as the exclusive forum for such review.

In its arguments to the Supreme Court, the administration invoked the Bush doctrine. It argued that the President has "inherent authority to convene military commissions to try and punish captured enemy combatants in wartime," even without congressional authorization, and that therefore the Court should be extremely hesitant to find that Bush's actions violated the law. And it insisted that in declaring that the Geneva Conventions did not apply to al-Qaeda Bush had exercised his constitutional war powers, and his decision was therefore "binding on the courts."

The Supreme Court's Ruling

The Supreme Court, by a vote of 5–3, rejected the President's contentions. (Chief Justice Roberts did not participate, since it was his own decision that was under review.) The Court's principal opinion was written by its senior justice, John Paul Stevens, a World War II veteran, and the only justice who has served in the military. He was joined in full by Justices [Ruth Bader] Ginsburg, [David] Souter, and [Stephen] Breyer, and in the main by Justice [Anthony] Kennedy. Kennedy also wrote a separate concurring opinion, and because he provided the crucial fifth vote, his views may prove more significant in the long run.

The Court found, first, that the administration's procedures for military tribunals deviated significantly from the court-martial procedures used to try members of our own armed forces, and that the Uniform Code of Military Justice barred such deviations unless it could be shown that court-martial procedures would be "impracticable." The administration made no such showing, the Court observed, and therefore the tribunals violated the limit set by Congress in the

Uniform Code. The Court could well have stopped there. This conclusion was a fully sufficient rationale to rule for Hamdan and invalidate the tribunals. Had it done so, the decision would have been far less consequential, since Congress could easily have changed its law or declared that court-martial procedures are impracticable.

But the Court went on to find that Congress had also required military tribunals to conform to the law of war, and that the tribunals impermissibly violated a particular law of war—Common Article 3 of the Geneva Conventions, which requires that detainees be tried by a "regularly constituted court affording all the judicial guarantees which are recognized as indispensable by civilized peoples."

Common Article 3 is denominated "common" because it appears in each of the four Geneva Conventions. It sets forth the basic human rights that apply to all persons detained in conflicts "not of an international character." The administration has long argued that because the struggle with al-Qaeda is international, not domestic, Common Article 3 does not apply. The Court rejected that view, explaining that the phrase "not of an international character" was meant in its literal sense, to cover all conflicts not between nations, or "international" in character. (Conflicts between nations are covered by other provisions of the Geneva Conventions.) Since the war with al-Qaeda is a conflict between a nation and a nonstate force, the Court ruled, it is "not of an international character," and Common Article 3 applies. . . .

The fact that the Court decided the case at all in the face of Congress's efforts to strip the Court of jurisdiction is remarkable in itself. That the Court then broke away from its history of judicial deference to security claims in wartime to rule against the President, not even pausing at the argument that the decisions of the commander in chief are "binding on the courts," suggests just how troubled the Court's majority was by the President's assertion of unilateral executive power.

That the Court relied so centrally on international law in its reasoning, however, is what makes the decision truly momentous.

Implications of the Decision

The *Hamdan* decision has sweeping implications for many aspects of the Bush doctrine, including military tribunals, NSA [National Security Agency] spying, and the interrogation of al-Qaeda suspects. With respect to trying alleged war criminals, the administration now has two options. Without changing the law, it can put into effect the regular court-martial procedures that are used for trying members of the American military. The administration has already rejected that option, and has instead said that it will ask Congress for explicit approval of military tribunals that afford defendants fewer protections than courts-martial would. Because the Court's decision rests on statutory grounds, the President could in theory seek legislation authorizing the very procedures that the Court found wanting. Already, Senators Jon Kyl, Lindsay Graham, Arlen Specter, and others have announced that they will seek legislation to authorize military tribunals.

But because the Court also ruled that Common Article 3 of the Geneva Conventions applies, and that the tribunals as currently constituted violate that provision, legislative reform is not so simple. Were Congress to approve the tribunals in their present form, it would thereby be authorizing a violation of Common Article 3. Congress unquestionably has the legal power, as a matter of domestic law, to authorize such a violation. Treaties and legislation are said to be of the same stature, and therefore Congress may override treaties by enacting superseding laws. But passing a law that blatantly violates a treaty obligation is no small matter. And the US has a strong interest in respecting the Geneva Conventions, since they protect our own soldiers when captured abroad. It is one thing to put forward an arguable interpretation of the treaty, as the administration did in contending that Common Article 3 simply did not apply in Hamdan's case. It is another thing to blatantly violate the treaty. As a result, the *Hamdan* decision is likely to force the administration to make whatever procedures it adopts conform to the dictates of Common Article 3. . . .

The most far-reaching implications of the Court's decision, however, concern the interrogation of al-Qaeda suspects. The administration has since the outset of the conflict sought to evade the limitations set by international law on coercive interrogation, reasoning that the need for "actionable intelligence" trumps the human dignity of its detainees. According to a January 25, 2002, memo from then White House Counsel Alberto Gonzales to the President, the desire to extract information from suspects was a prime motivating factor behind the administration's decision that the Geneva Conventions do not apply to the conflict with al-Qaeda. . . .

The *Hamdan* decision, while not explicitly addressed to the question of interrogation, should resolve this debate. Common Article 3 of the Geneva Conventions, which the Court has now authoritatively declared applies to the conflict with al-Qaeda, requires that all detainees be "treated humanely," and protects them against "outrages upon personal dignity, in particular humiliating and degrading treatment." Moreover, the federal War Crimes Act makes it a felony, punishable in some instances by death, to violate Common Article 3 in any way. Thus, CIA and military interrogators are now on notice that any inhumane treatment of a detainee subjects them to prosecution as a war criminal. While they might be confident that the Bush administration would not prosecute them, they cannot be sure that a future administration would overlook such war crimes. And it is quite possible that government officials might actually decide not to commit war crimes—now that they know they are war crimes—even if prosecution is unlikely. . . .

Some members of Congress have specifically objected to the implications of the Court's reliance on Common Article 3, and have suggested that they might try to undo it. Senator Graham has complained that the Court's ruling might make our soldiers liable for war crimes. But if American soldiers commit war crimes, they should be held responsible. Congress only recently passed the McCain Amendment's ban on all cruel, inhuman, and degrading treatment by overwhelming margins. Surely the last message we should want to send to the rest of the world is that the McCain Amendment was only for show, because we are not actually willing to be bound by these rules if they have any enforceable effect.

In fact, the Court's decision further suggests that President Bush has *already* committed a war crime, simply by establishing the military tribunals and subjecting detainees to them. As noted above, the Court found that the tribunals violate Common Article 3, and under the War Crimes Act, any violation of Common Article 3 is a war crime. Military defense lawyers responded to the *Hamdan* decision by requesting a stay of all tribunal proceedings, on the ground that their own continuing participation in those proceedings might constitute a war crime. But according to the logic of the Supreme Court, the President has already committed a war crime. He won't be prosecuted, of course, and probably should not be, since his interpretation of the Conventions was at least arguable. But now that his interpretation has been conclusively rejected, if he or Congress seeks to go forward with tribunals or interrogation rules that fail Article 3's test, they, too, would be war criminals.

The Role of International Law

Some have argued that the Court's decision in *Hamdan* was limited, because it rested on statutory rather than on constitutional grounds, and thereby left the door open for Congress to respond. But in choosing to decide the case despite Congress's apparent attempt to divest the Court of jurisdiction, in holding that the President is bound by congressional limitations even when acting as commander in chief, and most importantly in declaring that Common Article 3 governs the conflict with al-Qaeda, the Court's decision is anything but restrained. It is a potent refutation of the Bush doctrine, and a much-needed resurrection of the rule of law.

This lesson is especially clear when *Hamdan* is read in conjunction with the Court's decisions [in 2004] in the "enemy combatant" cases. In those cases, also clear defeats for the President, the Court rejected the administration's arguments that prisoners at Guantánamo had no right of access to federal courts to challenge the legality of their detention, and that US citizens held as "enemy combatants" had no right to a hearing to challenge whether they were in fact "enemy combatants." The administration's lawyers had put forward the Bush doctrine there, too, arguing that it would be unconstitutional for Congress or the courts to interfere with the President's unilateral power as commander in chief to detain the enemy. But the Court rejected that view, insisting that

> whatever power the United States Constitution envisions for the Executive in its exchanges with other nations or with enemy organizations in times of conflict, it most assuredly envisions a role for all three branches when individual liberties are at stake.

The *Hamdan* decision confirms not only that all three branches have a role to play, but that international law itself has an essential role, in particular the laws of war that the administration has for so long sought to evade. . . .

Making US practice conform to the international rules that formally reflect world opinion is a necessary first step if we are to begin to reduce the unprecedented levels of anti-American sentiment found among our allies and foes alike, and offset the propaganda advantage our unilateral approach has given to al-Qaeda.

The Bush doctrine views the rule of law as our enemy, and claims it is allied with terrorism. As the Pentagon's 2005 National Defense Strategy put it:

> Our strength as a nation state will continue to be challenged by those who employ a strategy of the weak using international fora, judicial processes, and terrorism.

In fact, both the strength and security of the nation in the struggle with terrorists rest on adherence to the rule of law, including international law, because only such adherence provides the legitimacy we need if we are to win back the world's respect. *Hamdan* suggests that at least one branch of the United States government understands this.

Congress Removed the Courts' Power to Set Policy in the War on Terror

John Yoo

John Yoo is a professor at the University of California–Berkeley Law School and the author of several books. He served in the Office of Legal Counsel at the U.S. Department of Justice from 2001 to 2003. In the following viewpoint, he points out that a new law passed by Congress following the Supreme Court's decision in Hamdan v. Rumsfeld *was a rebuke to the Court and an insistence that it not interfere with war policy. In Yoo's opinion, decisions concerning the war on terror should be made by Congress and the president, not the courts, which are ill-equipped to deal with military issues.*

During the bitter controversy over the military commission bill, which President [George W.] Bush signed into law [in October 2006], most of the press and the professional punditry missed the big story. In the struggle for power between the three branches of government, it is not the presidency that "won." Instead, it is the judiciary that lost.

The new law is, above all, a stinging rebuke to the Supreme Court. It strips the courts of jurisdiction to hear any habeas corpus claim filed by any alien enemy combatant anywhere in the world. It was passed in response to the effort by

John Yoo, "Sending a Message—Congress to Courts: Get Out of the War on Terror," *Wall Street Journal*, October 19, 2006. Copyright © 2006 Dow Jones & Company, Inc. All rights reserved. Reprinted with permission of The Wall Street Journal.

a five-justice majority in *Hamdan v. Rumsfeld* to take control over terrorism policy. That majority extended judicial review to Guantanamo Bay, threw the Bush military commissions into doubt, and tried to extend the protections of Common Article 3 of the Geneva Conventions to al Qaeda and Taliban detainees, overturning the traditional understanding that Geneva does not cover terrorists, who are not signatories nor "combatants" in an internal civil war under Article 3.

Hamdan was an unprecedented attempt by the court to rewrite the law of war and intrude into war policy. The court must have thought its stunning power grab would go unchallenged. After all, it has gotten away with many broad assertions of judicial authority before. This has been because Congress is unwilling to take a clear position on controversial issues (like abortion, religion or race) and instead passes ambiguous laws which breed litigation and leave the power to decide to the federal courts.

Until the Supreme Court began trying to make war policy, the writ of habeas corpus had never been understood to benefit enemy prisoners in war. The U.S. held millions of POWs [prisoners of war] during World War II, with none permitted to use our civilian courts (except for a few cases of U.S. citizens captured fighting for the Axis). Even after hostilities ended, the justices turned away lawsuits by enemy prisoners seeking to challenge their detention. In *Johnson v. Eisentrager,* the court held that it would not hear habeas claims brought by alien enemy prisoners held outside the U.S., and refused to interpret the Geneva Conventions to give new rights in civilian court against the government. In the case of Gen. Tomoyuki Yamashita, the court refrained from reviewing the operations of military commissions.

In *Hamdan,* the court moved to sweep aside decades of law and practice so as to forge a grand new role for the courts to open their doors to enemy war prisoners. Led by John Paul Stevens and abetted by Anthony Kennedy, the majority ignored or creatively misread the court's World War II precedents. The approach catered to the legal academy, whose tastes run to swashbuckling assertions of judicial supremacy and radical innovations, rather than hewing to wise but boring precedents.

Courts Must Not Decide Military Issues

Thoughtful critics point out that because the enemy fights covertly, the risk of detaining the innocent is greater. But so is the risk of releasing the dangerous. That's why enemy combatants who fight out of uniform, such as wartime spies, have always been considered illegals under the law of war, not entitled to the same protections given to soldiers on the battlefield or ordinary POWs. Disguised suicide-bombers in an age of WMD [weapons of mass destruction] proliferation and virulent America-hatred are more immediately dangerous than the furtive information-carriers of our Cold War past. We now know that more than a dozen detainees released from Guantanamo have rejoined the jihad [war against America]. The real question is how much time, energy and money should be diverted from winning the fight toward establishing multiple layers of review for terrorists. Until *Hamdan*, nothing in the law of war ever suggested that enemy status was anything but a military judgment.

While there may be different ways to strike a balance, this is a decision for the president and Congress, not the courts. The Constitution gives Congress the authority to determine the jurisdiction of federal courts in peacetime, and also declares that habeas corpus can be suspended "in Cases of Rebellion or Invasion" when "the public Safety may require it." Congress's power is even greater when it is correcting the justices' errors. Courts are ill-equipped to decide whether vast resources should be devoted to reviewing military detentions. Or whether military personnel's time should be consumed traveling back to the U.S. for detainee hearings. Or whether we risk revealing information in these hearings that might compromise the intelligence sources and methods that may allow us to win the war.

This time, Congress and the president did not take the court's power grab lying down. They told the courts, in effect, to get out of the war on terror, stripped them of habeas jurisdiction over alien enemy combatants, and said there was nothing wrong with the military commissions. It is the first time since the New Deal that Congress had so completely divested the courts of power over a category of cases. It is also the first time since the Civil War that Congress saw fit to narrow the court's habeas powers in wartime because it disagreed with its decisions.

The law goes farther. It restores to the president command over the management of the war on terror. It directly reverses *Hamdan* by making clear that the courts cannot take up the Geneva Conventions. Except for some clearly defined war crimes, whose prosecution would also be up to executive discretion, it leaves interpretation and enforcement of the treaties up to the president. It even forbids courts from relying on foreign or international legal decisions in any decisions involving military commissions.

All this went overlooked during the fight over the bill by the media, which focused on Sens. [John] McCain, [Lindsay] Graham and [John] Warner's opposition to the administration's proposals for the use of classified evidence at terrorist trials and permissible interrogation methods. In its eagerness to magnify an intra-GOP [inside the Republican Party] squabble, the media mostly ignored the substance of the bill, which gave current and future administrations, whether Democrat or Republican, the powers needed to win this war.

Organizations to Contact

The editors have compiled the following list of organizations concerned with the issues debated in this book. The descriptions are derived from materials provided by the organizations. All have publications or information available for interested readers. The list was compiled on the date of publication of the present volume; the information provided here may change. Be aware that many organizations take several weeks or longer to respond to inquiries, so allow as much time as possible.

American Civil Liberties Union (ACLU)
125 Broad St., 18th Fl., New York, NY   10004
(212) 549-2500
Web site: www.aclu.org

The American Civil Liberties Union is a large nonprofit organization that works in courts, legislatures, and communities to defend and preserve the individual rights and liberties that the Constitution and laws of the United States guarantee. Its Web site contains many articles on *Hamdan v. Rumsfeld* (in which it filed an amicus curiae brief) and also some on conscientious objectors.

Central Committee for Conscientious Objectors (CCCO)
405 Fourteenth St., Ste. 205, Oakland, CA   94612
e-mail: ccco@objector.org
Web site: www.objector.org

The Central Committee for Conscientious Objectors has been in operation since 1948. It works toward helping military personnel in trouble, educating the public about militarism and supporting individual and collective efforts to stop the spread of militarism. Its Web site contains arguments for conscientious objection and a detailed document, "Advice for Conscientious Objectors in the Armed Forces."

Central Intelligence Agency (CIA)
Office of Public Affairs, Washington, DC   20505
(703) 482-0623 • fax: (703) 482-1739
Web site: www.foia.cia.gov/rosenberg.asp

The CIA's online collection of files on the Rosenberg case includes documents that cover, among many other topics, U.S. intelligence activities, including FBI-CIA cooperation; Soviet intelligence activities; the Rosenberg espionage network's collection against the U.S. atomic energy program; their attempts to protect the network as U.S. authorities closed in on it; their arrest; Soviet propaganda; the Soviets' protest of the Rosenberg's sentencing; and Moscow's reaction to the execution of their spies.

Heart Mountain, Wyoming Foundation (HMWF)
PO Box 547, Powell, WY   82435
(307) 754-2689 • fax: (307) 754-0119
e-mail: pwolfe@wavecom.net
Web site: www.heartmountain.us

The Heart Mountain, Wyoming Foundation is a nonprofit organization established to memorialize and to educate the public about the significance of the historical events surrounding the internment of Japanese Americans at the Heart Mountain Relocation Center near Powell, Wyoming, between 1942 and 1945. Its Web site offers detailed information about Heart Mountain and about the history of the evacuation of Japanese Americans from the West Coast during World War II.

Internment Archives
e-mail: sam@internmentarchives.com
Web site: www.internmentarchives.com

This site contains an archive of more than four hundred documents, mostly primary sources, dealing with the reasons for the evacuation of Japanese Americans from the West Coast during World War II. It aims to present evidence that "it didn't happen the way it is told in the popular press, on radio and TV, and in hundreds of exhibits and displays around the country," and that the official investigation conducted in the 1980s ignored declassified intelligence showing that there was a real threat.

Japanese American Citizens League (JACL)
1765 Sutter St., San Francisco, CA 94115
(415) 921-5225 • fax: (415) 931-4671
e-mail: jacl@jacl.org
Web site: www.jacl.org

The Japanese American Citizens League is the oldest and largest Asian American civil rights organization in the United States. Its mission is to secure and maintain the civil rights of Japanese Americans and all others who are victimized by injustice and bigotry, and it also works to promote cultural, educational, and social values and to preserve the heritage and legacy of the Japanese American community. Its Web site contains information about Japanese American history, including a map of the World War II internment camps.

Japanese American National Museum (JANM)
369 E. First St., Los Angeles, California 90012
(213) 625-0414 • fax: (213) 625-1770
Web site: www.janm.org

The mission of the Japanese American National Museum is to promote understanding and appreciation of America's ethnic and cultural diversity by sharing the Japanese American experience. It believes in the importance of remembering Japanese American history to better guard against the prejudice that threatens liberty and equality in a democratic society. Its online collections include diaries and art describing the life of Japanese Americans in World War II internment camps.

National Committee to Reopen the Rosenberg Case
244 Fifth Ave., Ste. V-226, New York, NY 10001
(212) 252-2165

e-mail: rosenbergcommittee@gmail.com
Web site: www.rosenbergtrial.org

This organization seeks to have the Rosenbergs exonerated and to have the government publicly address and own up to its complicity in what the committee considers a terrible miscarriage of justice. Its Web site contains a detailed history of the case against the Rosenbergs, the trial, and their execution.

Peace Abbey Multi–Faith Retreat Center
2 N. Main St., Sherborn, MA   01770
(508) 655-2143 • fax: (508) 376-6246
e-mail: info@peaceabbey.org
Web site: www.peaceabbey.org

The Peace Abbey Multi–Faith Retreat Center is dedicated to creating innovative models for society that empower individuals on the paths of nonviolence, peacemaking, and cruelty-free living. It maintains a National Registry of Conscientious Objectors (CO) at its Web site, which contains articles about conscientious objection to war and personal stories of some COs.

For Further Research

Books

Alan I. Bigel, *Supreme Court on Emergency Powers, Foreign Affairs and Protection of Civil Liberties, 1935–75.* Lanham, MD: University Press of America, 1986.

Roger Daniels, *Prisoners Without Trial: Japanese Americans in World War II.* New York: Hill and Wang, 1993.

J.L. DeWitt, *Final Report: Japanese Evacuation from the West Coast, 1942.* Washington, DC: U.S. Government Printing Office, 1943.

Gerald R. Gioglio, *Days of Decision: An Oral History of Conscientious Objectors in the Military During the Vietnam War.* Trenton, NJ: Broken Rifle Press, 1989.

Lawson Fusao Inada, ed., *Only What We Could Carry: The Japanese American Internment Experience.* San Francisco: Heyday Books, 2000.

Peter H. Irons, *Justice at War: The Story of the Japanese American Internment Cases.* Berkeley and Los Angeles: University of California Press, 1993.

———, *War Powers: How the Imperial Presidency Hijacked the Constitution.* New York: Metropolitan Books, 2005.

Jennifer M. Lowe, ed., *The Supreme Court and the Civil War.* Washington, DC: Supreme Court Historical Society, 1996.

Jonathan Mahler, *The Challenge*: Hamdan v. Rumsfeld *and the Fight over Presidential Power.* New York: Farrar, Straus, and Giroux, 2008.

Michelle Malkin, *In Defense of Internment: The Case for Racial Profiling in World War II and the War on Terror.* Washington, DC: Regnery, 2004.

Charles C. Moskos and John Whiteclay Chambers, *The New Conscientious Objection: From Sacred to Secular Resistance*. New York: Oxford University Press, 1993.

John Neville, *The Press, the Rosenbergs and the Cold War*. Westport, CT: Praeger, 1995.

Ronald Radosh and Joyce Milton, *The Rosenberg File*. New Haven, CT: Yale University Press, 1997.

William H. Rehnquist, *All the Laws but One: Civil Liberties in Wartime*. New York: Knopf, 1998.

Sam Roberts, *The Brother: The Untold Story of the Rosenberg Case*. New York: Random House, 2001.

Greg Robinson, *By Order of the President: FDR and the Internment of Japanese Americans*. Cambridge, MA: Harvard University Press, 2003.

Clinton Rossiter, *The Supreme Court and the Commander in Chief*. Ithaca, NY: Cornell University Press, 1976.

Ben Sherman, *Medic! The Story of a Conscientious Objector in the Vietnam War*. New York: Ballantine, 2004.

Geoffrey R. Stone, *Perilous Times: Free Speech in Wartime from the Sedition Act of 1798 to the War on Terrorism*. New York: Norton, 2004.

———, *War and Liberty: An American Dilemma: 1790 to the Present*. New York: Norton, 2007.

James W. Tollefson, *The Strength Not to Fight: Conscientious Objectors of the Vietnam War—in Their Own Words*. Washington, DC: Brassey's, 2000.

Mark Tushnet, ed., *The Constitution in Wartime: Beyond Alarmism and Complacency*. Durham, NC: Duke University Press, 2005.

Periodicals

Robert Alt, "The 'Good Guys' Won?!" *National Review*, July 5, 2006.

Matt Bai, "He Said No to Internment," *The New York Times Magazine*, December 25, 2005.

Megan Barnett, "Trial Without End: The Rosenbergs," *U.S. News & World Report*, January 27, 2003.

David Cole, "Korematsu II?" *The Nation*, December 8, 2003.

Geoffrey Gagnon, "The War Within," *Boston*, May 2007.

David J. Garrow, "Another Lesson from World War II Internments," *The New York Times*, September 23, 2001.

William Glaberson, "Prosecution States Its Case in First Guantanamo Trial," *The New York Times*, July 26, 2008.

Michael Griffin, "A Soldier's Decision," *America*, January 29, 2007.

Liz Halloran, "Rules for an Unruly New War," *U.S. News & World Report*, March 27, 2006.

Nat Hentoff, "Supreme Court Strikes Fear," *The Village Voice*, August 15, 2006.

Scott Horton, "Verdict on Hamdan," *Harper's*, August 7, 2008. www.harpers.org/archive/2008/08/hbc-90003374.

Michael Isikoff and Stuart Taylor Jr., "The Gitmo Fallout; The Fight over the Hamdan Ruling Heats Up," *Newsweek*, July 17, 2006

Ian Jones, "Pacifists Prepare for Possibility of Draft," *National Catholic Reporter*, October 19, 2001.

Arthur Kinoy, "Reflections on the Rosenbergs," *The Nation*, June 11, 1983.

Jonathan Mahler, "War Powers: Why This Court Keeps Rebuking This President," *The New York Times*, June 15, 2008.

Charles McKarry, "Early Cold War Spies Exposed," *American Heritage*, May 1999.

The Nation, "Rosenbergs Revisited," June 25, 1983.

National Review, "An Outrage," June 30, 2006.

The New York Times, "A Victory for the Rule of Law," June 30, 2006.

Michael E. Parrish, "Cold War Justice: The Supreme Court and the Rosenbergs," *American Historical Review*, October 1977.

Martin Peretz, "Red Dusk," *The New Republic*, October 8, 2008.

Matt Pressman, "Postscript," *Vanity Fair*, May 2009.

Jeremy Rabkin, "Not as Bad as You Think; The Court Hasn't Crippled the War on Terror," *The Weekly Standard*, July 17, 2006.

Eugene Robinson, "'Values' We Have to Hide Abroad," *The Washington Post*, September 8, 2006.

Bruce Shapiro, "The High Price of Conscience," *The Nation*, January 20, 1992.

Thomas Sowell, "Suicidal Hand-Wringing," *The Washington Times*, September 20, 2006.

Charles Swift, "The American Way of Justice," *Esquire*, March 2007.

Time, "Bad Landmark; Righting a Racial Wrong," November 21, 1983.

———, "Mercy and Justice," February 23, 1953.

———, "The Rosenberg Myth," February 24, 1967.

The Washington Post, "Let There Be Law," July 2, 2006.

Index